TENDER
TIDE

A Willow Bay Novel

by Laurie Ryan

www.laurieryanauthor.com

COPYRIGHT

Tender Tide, Book 4 of the Willow Bay series, Copyright © 2022 Laurie Ryan All rights reserved
ebook ISBN: 9978-1-7358773-9-6
Print ISBN: 979-8-9859122-0-3

Editor: Libby Doyle, Fairhill Editing
Cover design: C. Friesen at DefianceBooks.com

Learn more about Laurie Ryan and her books at **www.laurieryanauthor.com** and for up-to-date information about releases, please consider joining Laurie's **mailing list** through her website.

This book is a work of fiction. Names, characters, places, opinions, and incidents are either the product of the author's imagination or are used fictionally. Any resemblance to actual persons, living or dead, or to actual events is entirely coincidental.

No part of this text may be reproduced in any form without the express written permission of the author. Thank you for respecting the hard work of this author and not encouraging piracy of copyrighted materials. To obtain permission to use portions of this text, other than for review purposes, please contact **laurie@laurieryanauthor.com**

QUALITY CONTROL: We strive to produce error-free books, but even with all the eyes that see the story during the production process, slips get by. So please, if you find a typo or any formatting issues, please let us know at laurie@laurieryanauthor.com so that we may correct it. Thank you!

DEDICATION

To my readers, who keep me going. I've found my happy place at the ocean. I hope each and every one of you has found a place you can go to regroup, renew, and energize yourself.

Chapter One

Gladys Hawthorne sat in her gray leather recliner staring through the open brocade drapes at the September sunshine, so rare on the coast this time of year. After last winter's abundance of rain, no one in Willow Bay looked forward to winter. Summer had been a glorious respite from mud puddles and flooded roads. She, for one, did not look forward to traipsing around in the rain. Her old bones complained more these days than ever before and her bobbed white hair went frizzy at the first drop. Still, it was the only way to keep an eye on her town.

That's how she thought of Willow Bay—as hers. She'd moved here after her husband's death several years ago and had adopted the town. And the town had adopted her. Except its people had no idea who Gladys Hawthorne really was. To them, she was the local street person, always around, eyes wide open, always with an opinion on how the town should be run. She'd harangued Josh Morgan, Willow Bay's Mayor, more times than she could count, yet he continued to treat her like a friend and always asked after her welfare.

Did she have enough food? Did she want a place to sleep?

That wife of his, Dana, had helped him to relax. Gladys smiled, knowing she'd had a part in making that happen. Same with Bernie, the fiery redhead who owned Square Peg pizza parlor, and her husband, Paul. A few choice words in the right ears had gotten them together and now they were expecting a baby, just like Dana and Josh.

As for Dana's friend Aimi and Willow Bay's sheriff, that had been the dangerous one. A deluded stalker had come after Aimi and Jackson had been the only one who could keep her safe. And now they were planning their wedding. Gladys hadn't been able to help much with that one, but she'd done what she could. Love, once again, had prevailed.

A deep sense of satisfaction filled Gladys as she sipped her morning tea from a dainty, floral cup. Mornings were her favorite time of the day. So much promise. New problems to solve, people to help past their stubborn nature. Speaking of which…

Noise, like a toolbox closing, sounded behind her. Lucas Taylor walked from the kitchen into her light and airy sitting room, carrying said box. Construction and handyman work had certainly done right by the ex-marine. The man's tall frame had muscles in all the right places, honed for work, not for show. But show they did. She might be old, but she had eyes and could appreciate a handsome man. With that short, thick blond hair that stood on end more than lay flat and those startling blue eyes, Luke was the quintessential boy next door. Man, she corrected herself. No way anyone of any age could call him a boy.

Gladys tapped her lips with her forefinger as if shushing a child. Luke was also very much a loner, something Gladys had mused about for some time now. With all he did to help others, he should be surrounded by the love of a good partner. And she'd finally come up with a solution for that.

"Leak's all fixed, Gladys."

"Thank you. You're a good man to come spur of the moment." She stood up and patted his arm. "And for keeping my secret."

"When are you going to let Willow Bay in on this whole 'not really a street person' thing?"

"When I'm good and ready, Luke Taylor. And not a moment before."

He shook his head. "You are an enigma, Miss Gladys. Not sure I'll ever understand you."

"Just keep fixing what breaks around here and we'll get along just fine." She pulled some cash out of her housecoat pocket and handed it to him.

"I don't like taking your money."

"If you don't start taking more of it, you'll end up like my alter ego for real. You don't charge enough for what you do."

He shrugged, so Gladys dropped the subject and moved on to something much dearer to her heart. "So, how are your neighbors doing?"

"The Powters? As well as can be expected."

"That stroke of Katherine's was a close call, wasn't it?"

"Too close. They almost didn't get her to the hospital in time." The frown on Luke's face showed his concern. "And Ned's health isn't great, either, with that bad hip of his."

"I heard that their daughter has moved back home to help out."

Luke's eyes brightened for a moment and Gladys worked hard to keep her glee under wraps.

"Yep," he said.

"Jasmin was always such a lovely girl. I don't understand why she moved all the way to New York City." Gladys had lived there for years and it didn't hold a candle to the quiet, small-town life of Willow Bay.

Luke shrugged, the scowl firmly back on his face. "Some people need change."

"Yes, they do, don't they? Sometimes, a change like that helps you figure out where home really is."

Gladys met Luke's sharp gaze with satisfaction. She'd planted the seed. Now all she could do was pray it would grow. Maybe give it the occasional nudge, but too much interference would send both these introverts in opposite directions.

That couldn't happen. They were perfect for each other. So Gladys changed the subject to safer ground. "You going to the Cannery Park opening?"

"Yep. Want a ride?"

"Oh, no, dearie." She put a hand on his arm again and walked him to the back door. "Wouldn't do to have me seen on the arm of a hunk like you. Everybody would start thinking I'm off the market."

Luke's frown disappeared as he chuckled. "Like I said, you're an enigma." He reached down to kiss her cheek, then left with a wave, walking through her backyard at a casual pace. Because of her need for subterfuge, he would take the alley to the side street and walk around to his truck, which was parked several houses away.

"Such a good boy," she said, closing the door and heading for her bedroom. It was time to get dressed and out and about to see what was happening in her town today.

Chapter Two

After finishing up some minor maintenance on Willow Bay's blue and white striped lighthouse, Luke stood and looked out over the ocean. The waves were quiet today, as was the wind. There was no better view than this one right here, on the outer walkway of the lighthouse. Volunteering to maintain the building and its all-important light meant he could enjoy this view. He came here a lot, even when he wasn't working. He could think here. Process. Corral his emotions into some semblance of normalcy.

Calm the chaos in his mind.

Drawing a deep breath of salty air, he closed his eyes, raising his head to the sun. Fall had just begun and this warmth was unusual at the ocean this time of year. A gift he treasured. He didn't have much to do today now that he'd finished at Gladys's. Maybe he'd get his fishing pole and hit the beach. Try to nab some ocean surf perch for dinner. Might as well take advantage of the nice weather.

Gladys. Luke shook his head, unable to figure the woman out. She acted like a street person, yet lived in one of the most expensive mansions in town, right next to the mayor. Right under the man's nose and he didn't know. While curious about why she lived a covert life, Luke would never ask. It wasn't his place. The story behind this lady would come out in its own time. Until then, he'd keep her secret. Everyone had a right to their secrets, including him.

But she'd brought up something that had been on his mind a lot lately. Or someone. Jasmin Powter. They'd been raised as neighbors and he'd harbored a crush on the girl next door all through high school. She'd been all about leaving Willow Bay as soon as she could, which had intimidated the hell out of him. This was home and he didn't want to be anywhere else. By the time he told her he liked her, graduation loomed. They'd been great together—really great. Luke hadn't wanted it to end but her wanderlust came between them. She wasn't going to fulfill her dreams here in Willow Bay and he didn't want to live here without her, so he'd joined the Marines. He'd left first, just about the hardest thing he'd ever done. His departure gave her the opening she needed to stretch her wings and fly. He'd kept in touch as long as he could, but distance pulled them apart after she'd moved to New York City and their chats grew fewer and fewer until they disappeared altogether. Their paths hadn't crossed since. He'd been home a couple years now, wiser about the world and way more cynical at the ripe old age of twenty-seven. And living in the house he'd been raised in, right next door to the Powter place.

Now Jasmin was home and he couldn't stop thinking about the what-ifs. Luke shook his head, dispelling the thought. Too much had happened. He'd seen too much, done too much. Jasmin was an innocent compared to what he'd gone through. She didn't deserve a guy with PTSD and a string of nightmares to prove it.

Heading back in, Luke descended the steep lighthouse stairs. Time to stop feeling sorry for himself and get back to this nice weather. Locking the entry door behind him, he'd just thrown his toolbox in the back of his truck when he heard the clip-clop of horses' hooves. Before long, a train of eight horses and riders rounded the drive into the lighthouse, the lead horse being led by the subject of his thoughts.

Jasmin. He hadn't seen her since she'd arrived home. Luke checked in on her elderly folks at regular intervals, but she'd always been at the beach with the horses, the only source of income her parents had. Neither of them could ride anymore, so the job fell to their daughter.

Her long hair, tamed by a ponytail that twitched back and forth as she swung her head, matched the scowl on her face. She marched toward him, her helmet unstrapped, holding on to the horse's saddle as if to keep it in place. Those dark, stormy eyes looked like they'd cut him in half if he so much as moved an inch. But damned if she wasn't the most beautiful thing he'd set eyes on in a long, long time. Old yearnings reared up in Luke. If they hadn't gone their separate ways, he knew he'd have been a one-woman man.

Reminding himself that Willow Bay wasn't her home, Luke pushed off from the side of the truck and met her in the middle of the parking lot, prepared for a less-than-warm greeting.

"No one dismounts," she said, turning back to the group. "Feel free to walk your horses around the parking lot while I deal with my saddle." She glanced at Luke. "Don't walk on the grass. This is Luke Taylor, the lighthouse keeper. We don't want to piss him off." She turned a grim smile Luke's way.

"Hey, Jazz. Long time."

"Hi." Her voice radiated frustration and anger.

"What's going on?"

"Damn saddle strap broke and I'm not sure how I'm going to get these folks, and my horses, back to the trailer if I can't ride."

"Let me take a look." He ran a hand along the neck of

the sleek quarter horse. Lexie had been Jasmin's horse since her sixteenth birthday and he'd fed her a lot of carrots since he'd been back.

"No sense. It's shredded. I knew it wasn't going to hold much longer but this is the last ride of the season and we can't afford a new saddle. Well, anyhow, it looks like I'll be the one hoofing it on the trip back to the trailers."

"I'd be happy to drop your saddle off for you."

"I can figure something out, thank you."

"Stubborn as always, eh?" he said, hoping for a smile.

Instead, he got a scowl. Man, was she prickly.

"At least let me check it out." He softened his voice, trying to soothe her into saying yes.

Jasmin looked away, then back at him. After a long moment, she muttered a "fine" and stepped back.

Lifting the flap, Luke fingered the leather. Jasmin was right, the strap was beyond repair, worn to threads right in the middle. He checked out both ends of the strap and thought he might be able to jury-rig something to at least get her back to the trailer.

Without saying a word, he walked to his truck and grabbed the tools he'd need. The other horses dutifully walked the edges of the parking lot like it was an arena, making him smile. Even strangers and horses followed Jasmin's orders.

Back beside the horse, Luke poked a hole in the top of the strap with an awl.

"Hey!" Jasmin said. "Don't destroy my saddle." She stepped closer and covered the strap with her hand.

"This strap is toast. I can't make it any worse, can I?" She only came up to his chin. He'd forgotten that. God, how could her hair smell so good? A flash, his fingers twining through her long strands, pulling her closer...

"Well, no, probably not, but— "

Luke shook his head to clear images he had no right to call to mind, even if he wanted to. Too often. "I think I have a fix that will get you back to the trailer." He settled an arm along the saddle.

"Well, all right. I'm hoping to get this fixed over the winter, though, so be gentle."

"Gentle is my middle name," he said, right back in those images of the two of them after high school.

When Jasmin blushed, Luke ducked his head to hide his smile. He widened the hole he'd started then reached down to unbuckle his belt. Jasmin's eyes widened.

"What are you doing?"

"Using my belt to get you home."

"Umm, okay. But it might not survive the trip."

He smiled. "That's okay. I have other belts."

After fixing the belt in place, Luke tugged on the strap. "Good as new. Well, almost. I wouldn't stand up in the saddle if I were you. And I'd mount carefully."

She raised her foot, but Luke stopped her. "The less stress, the better." He formed a cup by interlocking his fingers and leaned in to give Jasmin a leg up. When she didn't immediately move to mount, Luke glanced up to see her scowling. Again. He didn't know why she was so surly, but he waited and she finally moved toward him.

Jasmin smelled like her name, all exotic and spicy. He could get lost in that smell. Hell, he wanted to get lost, just like he had that summer. He wanted to do it all over again.

After she settled her boot in his hand, he lifted her into the saddle. Unable to resist, he ran a hand down Jasmin's calf and helped seat her foot to stirrup. He would have kept his hand there, propriety be damned, but Jasmin reined her horse and shifted away. Still, he'd noticed the intense flare in her eyes. Maybe she wasn't as unaffected by him as she tried to pretend.

Luke's smile widened as he brushed sand and dirt off his hands. And Jasmin's scowl deepened.

"All right, everyone," Jasmin said as her group gathered. "Time to get you all back to your four-wheeled rides. Kirsten?"

The youngest rider, probably about ten years old with a bright pink baseball jacket and blond braids peeking out beneath her helmet, came forward. "Yes?"

"Do you remember the way back to the trailer?"

"Yes, ma'am."

Jasmin squinted, probably at the word ma'am. "Then lead us out of here."

The girl's face lit up. "Come on, everyone. This way."

Everyone smiled as they followed Kirsten out of the parking area around the lighthouse.

Just before Jasmin followed, she turned back to Luke. "Thank you for the fix."

And for the minor feel? A smart man who tried to think before he spoke, Luke just nodded. "Anytime."

Jasmin stared at him for a moment longer, then trailed after her charges, back to the beach.

After they were out of sight, Luke got in his truck, mulling over what had just happened. Jasmin had not been happy to see him. While he didn't understand why, he couldn't quite keep the smile off his face as he drove to the beach, grabbed his fishing gear from the back of the truck, and headed for the water.

~~~

Jasmin loaded the last horse into the trailer, then undid the temporary hitching posts, hefting them into the bed of the old Chevy truck with an extra burst of energy. She sure could use that shiny black truck Luke drove. Jasmin hit the side of the '87 her parents had bought new. Of all the people to rescue her, it had to be Luke Taylor? The high school shy boy who'd leaped out of his self-imposed shell at graduation, almost too late. They'd had two amazing weeks together. Because of him, she'd almost scrapped a future that had nothing to do with Willow Bay. Then, with fourth of July fireworks going off all around them, he'd told her he was leaving the next day for the Marines. He'd never given a thought to her plans, her goals. She'd wanted Luke to come with her to New York. After he'd left, she had even less of a reason to stay in Willow Bay, so she'd lit out within a month, fulfilling her dream to move to New York City.

Turning the key in the ignition, Jasmin prayed the usual grinding sounds hadn't gotten worse.

In a wide, careful arc, she made her way off the hard-packed sand, easing onto the beach road as the truck groaned under the weight it pulled. Eight horses, tack, and various items loaded in a trailer way past its prime, same as the truck. How had her parents let things get so bad in just a few short years? Nary a word to worry her each time she called them. If they'd told her things were so dire, she could have helped, sent them money. Though not much, because she'd barely managed to make ends meet living in an apartment with six other people. New York was an expensive place to live.

Her parents were proud people who didn't want help from anyone, even their daughter apparently, until things were almost too far gone. This realization couldn't have come at a worse time. Working for Altair Clothing, an online clothing sales outlet, she'd talked her boss into letting her redesign their website. She'd spent four months creating the perfect online storefront for the business. She'd been offered a promotion, one that meant she could maybe move to a new place and only have a couple of roommates. Then her mother had a devastating stroke and Jasmin hadn't thought twice. She'd quit her job, packed up everything, and come home, worry for her mother at war with her resentment over having to move back to Willow Bay. Family trumped everything else. Jasmin knew that and believed it in her soul, but she'd loved her New York life. Leaving it behind was a hard pill to swallow. Even worse, her resentment had grown every day since.

Pulling into the Powter property now, Jasmin saw it for what it was. Borderline dump. Everything her parents earned went toward keeping the horses fed and housed. The house needed a new roof and windows, the weathered boards needed painting. The outbuildings and equipment weren't much better. Now that fall had arrived and she didn't have to be at the beach every day offering rides to tourists, she could dredge up some of her carpenter skills from high school summer work and fix this place up a bit.

Not that she was looking forward to it. Jasmin parked by the corral attached to the barn, walked to the back of the trailer and opened the gate. After the horses backed into the corral, she unloaded all the tack and equipment. She'd have to go over everything, oil the saddles to keep the leather supple through the winter months. And get that damn saddle fixed. She dumped it on the tack room floor. Tomorrow was soon enough for that. She was bone tired.

One by one, she led the horses into their stalls and fed them, finishing up with Lexie.

"Come on, girl. You get to rest now. Not me. No sir." She glanced at the house. "No rest for the weary."

Lexie nudged her shoulder as if she understood. With a smile, Jasmin quickly brushed her down, fed her, swept sand out of the trailer, then parked the truck and headed to the porch. She sank into one of the old wicker chairs. Ned Powter, her father, sat in the other one, his dark hair so much grayer these days. His weathered face and tired eyes watched Jasmin as she pulled off her boots and sank back into the cushions.

"How was today?" he asked.

"Slow, but I got three good runs in. Saddle broke while we were out on the last one."

"How'd you get back?"

"Luke Taylor fixed it."

Her father's bushy eyebrows shot up.

"How's Mom?" Jasmin said, not wanting to give her father any time to think on the subject of Luke Taylor. Her parents had worried, that summer, about her instant devotion to Luke. Little had they known she'd crushed on him for a long time before graduation. Or that he was the one person who might have kept her in Willow Bay.

Eyeing his daughter, Ned paused to take a draw off his pipe before speaking. "Your mother still doesn't want to get out of bed."

"Did you make her?"

"How?"

"Damn it, Dad. We talked about this." Jasmin shoved her boots next to the chair and stood. "She's never going to improve if she doesn't get up. I can't be in two places at once. You *have* to get her to do her exercises."

Yanking open the screen door, Jasmin glanced at her father, a man once larger than life who now had shrunk into a tiny shell of himself. She let the screen door slam shut and knelt in front of him, tears filling her eyes. "I'm so sorry, Dad. I know you're doing your best."

He tugged a strand of hair dislodged from her ponytail. "We're all doing the best we can. And you are working harder than any of us when you don't even want to be here. I'm sorry, bug."

Jasmin smiled at the nickname she used to hate. "I'm where I need to be. We'll get through this." With a deep breath, she hugged her father and went inside. The kitchen walls were a dingy yellow that needed updating, as did the eyelet curtains that used to be white. Late afternoon autumn sunshine did little to cheer the room up, but Jasmin barely noticed as she turned into the dark master bedroom off the kitchen, which used to be her room. How many times had her mother opened this very door to wake Jasmin up, her face a portrait of joy and love? Now, it was her mother's room because it was on the main floor. Jasmin steeled herself for the battle to come.

"Mom? You awake?"

No answer, except for bed covers shifting.

Jasmin pulled the blackout shades aside, letting in what was left of the day's sunshine.

"Owwww," her mother cried, covering her eyes. "Hurts."

Had the word come out clearer than last time? It was hard to tell. Her mother's aphasia had, so far, not responded to speech therapy. If she would practice at home, she'd get better faster. Getting her mother to exercise anything these days was a test of patience. Seeing her mother so defeated made Jasmin want to cry. Katherine Powter wasn't old, only sixty-four. Too young to have been taken down by such a debilitating stroke. Jasmin had been a late-in-life baby. She'd known she'd have to help her parents sooner than most of her friends, but she hadn't figured on that day coming this early. But family was family.

Putting on her brightest smile, Jasmin leaned down and kissed her mother's forehead, brushing her reddish-gray hair back from her face. "Hey, that came out nice and clear. You did good."

"Ugh." Her mother waved a dismissive hand at Jasmin and looked away.

"Nope. No looking away, Mom. We need to get you out of this bed for a while."

"No."

"Yes."

Her mother turned back and glared at Jasmin, proving once again that she could show emotion when she wanted to.

"Mom, you'll get sores if you don't get out of bed. Now come on." Jasmin pulled the covers aside, or tried to. Her mother held on tight with her good arm. This was the fight they had every single day. Her mother wanted to give up, her father gave in to her mother's wishes, and Jasmin fought the battles.

"You are getting into the wheelchair." Jasmin pulled the chair into position by the bed and then straightened the pad that helped cushion tender skin. Giving her mother no chance to argue, she pulled the covers back, put one arm under her mother's knees and the other one around her shoulders, then swung her mother around to sit on the side of the bed.

"No no no," her mother mumbled, slapping at Jasmin's arm.

"Sorry, Mom. Doc says you need to get up, so you're getting up. It's almost dinner time, so you can eat at the table with us."

"No no no," her mother cried, tears forming in her eyes.

Jasmin bit her lip to keep her own tears at bay. Forcing her mother to get out of bed against her will. Could this get any harder?

Once her mother was settled in the chair, Jasmin tucked a lap blanket over her to keep her warm in the drafty house, then reached for the hairbrush. As she stroked her mother's tangles into some semblance of order, Jasmin began to hum one of the songs her mother used to sing. When she finished and pulled the hair up into a soft bun, Jasmin knelt in front of her mother.

"I miss your singing."

Her mother, calmer now, lifted her good hand and touched Jasmin's cheek.

"I know you miss it, too, Mom. And I'm sorry I have to be this way, but I'm not ready to let you go. If you won't fight to get better, I'll fight for you." Tears stung her eyes once more at the misery on her mother's face.

"Can you just say one new word today? Maybe you could tell me what you want for dinner."

Her mother moved her mouth, opened it, closed it without uttering a sound, and looked away again.

Damn. Jasmin stood and covered her trembling lips with her hand. This was so hard. When she knew she could keep the tears from falling, she wheeled her mother out to the living room and turned on her favorite soap opera. "You rest here. I'll get you something to drink."

She brought back some water, setting it on a table where her mother could reach it with her working hand, then went to get dinner going. Her father had already started fried chicken and mashed potatoes. If Jasmin kept eating like this, she'd be a two-hundred-pound cholesterol junkie in no time.

Opening the fridge door, she pulled lettuce out. "I'll make a salad."

"Why?" her father said. "She won't eat it."

"I will, and I'll keep trying." She leaned on the counter, wondering how she could get through to her mother.

Her father patted her on the back. "We both will, bug. We both will. I should have made her get up."

"We're doing the best we can." Jasmin hugged him.

After dinner and getting her mother settled in for the night, Jasmin poured a glass of her father's homemade wine and went out to sit on the porch. Ned Powter's wine was legendary among the locals of Willow Bay. He'd taken the art form to a new level but refused to do more than bottle it for friends and neighbors. He didn't know it yet, but Jasmin had sent a few bottles into a competition, just to see how they would test alongside other wines. She hoped to hear soon if it made the finals. If it did, and she could convince her father to bottle commercially, it might generate some desperately needed income. Ride sales and her parent's social security didn't get them through the month and her own meager savings was about gone.

Pulling her boots on, Jasmin wandered out to the barn, wine in hand, to make sure the horses were good for the night, stopping by each stall to give them a pat and a kind word. There were so many empty stalls. Her father had sold half their stock to keep the place going. Jezebel, Hinky, Thomas—all were gone now. Only ten horses remained, something that both relieved and saddened Jasmin. How had her parents let things get so bad?

Except it hadn't been just her parents. She'd dropped the ball, too, settling into her life in New York a little too deeply and never taking the time to read between the lines when she spoke to them. She should have known. They were aging. Taking care of this place took a lot of strength and time.

That's why she'd come home so quickly. Guilt. That had eventually faded, but she couldn't leave them unless she could talk them into selling the place. She'd broached the subject with her father and he'd shut her down immediately. Wouldn't even consider the possibility.

"This is our home. We're staying put," he'd said. And that had been the end of that.

Jasmin tried to corral her frustration, but sometimes it wasn't easy. The wine lulled her into a more tranquil mood as she moved down the row of horses to the small office they kept in the barn. Covered in dust when she'd first arrived home, the office had been the first place she'd cleaned up. This was where she could think, could breathe, could let everything from one day go and get ready for the next. This is where, if she ever got the chance, she would get back to web design. Though she'd need internet to do that. At the moment, she didn't have the money.

Right now, what she needed was a plan. And a budget. Setting her wine glass down on the desk blotter, she reached for a pad and pen and started writing down everything that needed to be done so she could prioritize. Once she did that, she'd work on where to get the money for all of it.

Because if her parents wanted to stay here, it was up to her to make that happen.

Chapter Three

Luke stood in the barn office doorway watching Jasmin concentrate while she wrote. It had surprised him, how strongly he'd reacted to the sight of her. Yes, he'd crushed on her in high school, but that had gone unrequited until just before graduation. He had to admit, memories from that summer had gotten him through some tough times.

Jasmin glanced up, then jumped, pushing back from the desk.

"Shit, Luke. You scared me," she said, settling back into place.

"Sorry. Just wanted to make sure the saddle got you home."

She held her arms out to each side. "Home, safe and sound."

"Good." He leaned against the door.

"You always come on the property without permission?"

He shrugged. "Been doing it for a while, keeping an eye on things."

"Before I got home?" Jasmin's brows drew together. Luke wanted to smooth them. He nodded, walked in, and settled into a chair across the desk from her.

"Oh, my God, you found Mom that day."

That had been rough. Luke tapped his toes on the floor as he remembered the panic, his brain trying to sort through his rudimentary first aid skills. Trying to calm his own racing heart so he could help Katherine.

"Would you, uh..." Jasmin met his eyes and took a breath. "Would you tell me about that day?"

Luke looked around the room, at all the pictures. Jasmin's mother riding, singing karaoke, taking pictures, smiling. So many memories. He liked to think of her that way, not like she was now. But reality was a bear that he sometimes had to look in the face.

"I'd come over to check on a leak I'd fixed. Found her in the yard. Breathing, heart beating, but unconscious. I called 911. They arrived pretty quickly, stabilized her, and whisked her off to the hospital. But the damage was done."

"Dad wasn't home?"

"No. He was on the beach leading rides. I found him just after he got back. I gave him my truck and sent him to the hospital. Then I got the horses back to the stable and joined him."

Luke stood up and walked to the lone window, looking out over the yard, still very aware of the spot where he'd found Katherine. "Your dad had called you by then. Still, it was a long night, waiting to hear if she'd make it."

He heard Jasmin get up. Before long, she stood beside him, looking out the same window. He breathed in her spicy, soothing scent.

"You stayed through the night?" she whispered.

Turning to her, Luke nodded. "You were on your way. I stayed until we knew. Until Ned could draw a breath."

"Then you probably came back and fed the horses, didn't you?"

"Needed to be done."

Her eyes were so dark, like the deep cherry tone that gave wood a depth of character. He wanted to touch her, to kiss her. Before he could, she threw her arms around him, hugging him tight.

"Thank you. For being there. Mom's alive because you got her care."

Luke hugged her back, loving the feel of her against him, breathing deeply of her scent. God, she felt good.

As quickly as the hug began, it ended. Jasmin moved away, settled back in her chair, and pushed it back like she needed as much distance as possible.

"Would you like to go out sometime?" he asked, barely recognizing that he'd said the words out loud. Luke already missed the feel of her body against his.

The intensity of Jasmin's regard made him weak in the knees as he held his breath and waited.

"I don't think that's a good idea."

Ouch. With a stifled sigh, he headed for the door, not ready to hear her reasoning. He turned back briefly. "I'm glad you're home." Before he said any more of the words crowding his head, he left. Jasmin had so much on her plate right now, she didn't need him complicating things.

And he wanted that. Wanted her and her complications. Except he didn't have the right to ask. He was a shell of what he'd been. How could he expect anyone to buy into that?

Slowly, letting the dark of night envelope him in its own sense of serenity, Luke made his way back to his property. Opening the door to the small two-bedroom house he'd grown up in, he turned on the gas fireplace, settled into the recliner he slept in more nights than not, and stared at the flames, awash in memories. Some good, mostly horrible. Jasmin's mother, his own parents dying in that freak accident, the in-country incident he could never quite manage to forget.

All part of his life now, making reparations for his mistakes. If he'd gotten to Katherine sooner. If he'd been home when his parents decided to take off on that winter RV jaunt. If he hadn't left Aisha in that hut. Trying to heal what had broken him. Wishing his parents were there. God, the house was lonely without them. He'd never get used to not having them there. Never.

~~~

After Luke left, Jasmin downed the rest of her wine, barely tasting it. What was it about Luke Taylor that turned her into a pile of jelly? Hugging him had been a rash decision, one she now regretted. Not because he didn't deserve her gratitude. Because he'd felt good. Too good. And smelled even better, like freshly sanded wood. All those post-graduation memories flooded back to her. Being in his arms, laying with him in the barn. Her body warmed just thinking about it.

Then it all cooled as she considered the aftermath. Froze, more like it. He'd made her rethink everything in less than a month, then ripped it all away. Luke Taylor was nothing but complicated. With all the problems she had, she needed to remember that.

Picking up her pen, she tried to concentrate on the list she'd been prioritizing. After several minutes of staring at the pages, she gave up, turned off the lights, and headed for bed. Tomorrow was another day.

And, if she lay there remembering the feel of his body against hers, how she'd reacted physically to a simple hug, no one would blame her.

Right?

Chapter Four

Jasmin woke up grumpy. Not that unusual for her, but this morning, she was extra grumpy, having gotten less sleep than she would have liked thanks to long-buried memories and regrets. Damn it. She did not have time for this.

Pulling on jeans, a clean t-shirt, and a denim overshirt, she went downstairs and followed the smell of strong coffee to the kitchen. Her dad sat at the table nursing his cup, white with milk. Probably extra sweet, too.

"Morning," she said.

He waved a greeting. The smart man had quickly learned to wait for her caffeine to kick in before talking to her. Taking a long, appreciative whiff, Jasmin smiled. Black, leaded, and strong. Just how she liked it. She sank into a chair, noticing that her dad read something from a pad just like the one she'd been writing on in the barn.

"Lots here to do, it looks like."

Oh. He had her list.

"You've been out to the barn?"

He nodded. "Saw this. Brought it in so we could talk about it."

Jasmin took a sip of her coffee. "Everything on that list is stuff that should be done now."

"I agree. But we don't have the money to do it all."

"No, we don't. Which means we have to prioritize. Winterizing comes first."

"The horses come first."

Well, that's a given. "Of course, but everything with a star next to it needs to be done before the weather turns bad. I can do most of it. I'll start today."

Her dad held up the list. "This is a tall order with fall weather already knocking at the door."

Exactly what she'd thought last night. Jasmin shrugged. "We don't have much choice."

"Weather's not bad today," he said, looking off into the distance.

"That means it's a good day to start."

"Except I got a call last night. A request for a private party ride. Today."

Jasmin's heart fell. She didn't have time for this. "I hope you told them no."

"They made the offer too hard to resist."

Well, shit. "How many?"

"Only five, but probably a four-hour ride. A family wants to spread their father's ashes in a more isolated spot."

"Damn it." Jasmin got up and poured her coffee, which now tasted sour in her mouth, down the sink. "Kind of hard to argue with that."

"I can take them out."

"Not when you need a hip replacement, you can't." Jasmin worked hard to rein in her impatience and reset her plans for the day. "What time? I'll take them out."

"Eleven."

At least that gave her time to check supplies and prep for working on the roof tomorrow. The house needed a new roof, but for now, she'd have to apply tar to the worst spots and pray they could stay dry through the winter. They needed money. Maybe she could get a job now that they were done with rides. Or almost done. Maybe some temp work at Square Peg Pizza or the ice cream shop or Connie's C&C cafe. She'd add that to her list of things to look into and make it a priority.

She headed out to the truck, checked the gas, and pulled it into the yard. In the tack room, she kicked her own broken saddle and grabbed up what she needed. Once all the tack was loaded, she went to one of the three storage sheds on their acreage to look for roofing supplies. Hopefully, she'd have enough time to get up on the roof before dark and see exactly what needed to be done. The fact that they had extra shingles, tar paper, and tar paste meant it wouldn't cost her anything to do some fixes. That would be tomorrow's chore.

Back in the house, she bathed her mother and got her into the wheelchair. Always a battle, she made sure to finish with brushing and styling her mother's hair, something that always seemed to calm her.

"You got Mom while I'm gone?" she asked as she joined her dad in the kitchen.

"Yes. Maybe we'll go sit on the porch for a while this afternoon." He set a plate of bacon and eggs in front of Jasmin, who would have preferred healthier oatmeal and blueberries. She'd need the protein to get through the day, though, so she dug in as he took a plate out to the living room to help her mother eat.

Placing her empty plate in the sink, Jasmin grabbed her coat and hat, gave her parents kisses on their cheeks, and, affecting a cheerier attitude than she felt, headed out to the truck.

Luke leaned against it and her attitude hit the dirt.

"You're not done with rides?" he asked.

"One more. Special request. Ash spreading."

"Need any help? I've got the day free."

That was so not what she needed, spending the day with this man. Nope. Nope. Nope. Though a teensy part of her heart kept nudging her to say yes. "I've got it."

"M'kay." He glanced at the house. "Roof's in pretty bad shape. I could do some temporary fixes to get you through."

Was the guy looking for excuses to hang around? It would be so nice to have help, but Luke wasn't family. The Powters didn't accept charity. They could take care of themselves. "I've got that handled, too."

Luke's face briefly tightened. He pushed off the truck and stepped closer to Jasmin, making it hard for her to breathe. Her brain went completely dead when he tugged at a lock of hair she hadn't yet put in her usual ponytail.

"You don't have to do everything all by yourself, Jazz."

Jazz. When everyone else in high school called her Pouter Powter, he'd been the only person who'd refused. He'd come up with his own nickname for her. The wave of nostalgia almost sank her. Shoring up her backbone, Jasmin stared at him. "It's my job."

"You're not alone. Let me help."

Stepping back, she steeled herself. "Like you helped yourself to my heart before you left for the Marines?"

Luke flinched as if she'd slapped him. His jaw worked back and forth, opened as if he might speak, then closed. Finally, as Jasmin watched him squirm, he held up his hands. "I'm more sorry for that than you'll ever know. I should have told you sooner."

He turned and walked off, head down. Remorse filled Jasmin. She wanted to run after him and let him off the hook. Instead, she climbed into the truck and leaned her forehead on the steering wheel for a long moment. Then, with a glance in the rearview mirror to make sure Luke was gone, she pulled out onto the road and headed for the beach, her heart heavy.

~~~

Later that day, Luke walked over to the Powters on a mission, glad to see Jasmin's father on the front porch.

"Afternoon, Ned," Luke said as he shook the man's hand. "How are you?"

"The usual aches and pains. Nothing new."

"Katherine doing any better?"

Ned shook his head, his face a mixture of misery and pain. Luke patted him on the shoulder.

"Give her time."

"It's been months. She's given up and I don't know how to get through to her."

Based on Luke's own limited experience, he knew Katherine would have to choose to get better—for herself. That wouldn't help Ned or Jasmin feel better though. Luke had no answers for them, so he stuck to what he knew.

"Thought I'd take a look at patching that roof of yours," Luke said.

Ned pursed his lips. "That'd be nice of you. Jasmin said she'd do it, but we got a ride scheduled for today."

Luke nodded.

"Jasmin seemed pretty clear she'd do it herself. You might get some flack from her."

"Yep. Figured that."

Jasmin may have blown him off, but she needed help whether she knew it or not. He could give stubborn as well as she dished it out. Luke waved goodbye to Ned, helped himself to the necessary supplies, and climbed onto the Powter's roof.

The moss treatments he'd done had kept the vegetation in check, but the roof itself was in bad shape. He lifted the corner of a shingle and it broke off. Replacing the whole thing had to be beyond what they could handle financially, so Luke got to work tarring wherever it looked bad and replacing shingles where needed. He'd been at it a couple hours when he heard the truck drive into the yard.

Showtime.

"What the hell?"

Wow. She'd barely thrown the truck into park.

Luke stood up on the roof and stretched, working out kinks from the bent-over work. "Hey, Jazz." She looked good all fired up. Alive. Not that he wanted her angry at him, but he could see the fire in her eyes from here and remembered when that fire had turned to more pleasurable activities.

"What are you doing?" she said, her voice shaking with emotion.

"Fixing the roof."

"Fixing *my* roof."

"Technically, your parents' roof."

If steam could have poured out of her ears, it would have. He watched as she rounded the house and climbed the ladder, one stomping foot at a time. She marched right up to him and poked him in the chest with her finger.

"Ow."

"Get this straight, Lucas Taylor. I'm back now, and I don't need your charity. *We* don't need your charity."

He rubbed his chest. The woman had more strength in her finger than he'd given her credit for. "It's not charity—"

"Well, we're not paying you, so what else would you call it?"

"Being neighborly."

She chewed her lower lip so hard that Luke almost reached out to stop her. But he knew if he touched her lip, he'd want to do more.

"We don't need your help, Luke."

Okay, stubborn was getting to him. Stubborn, pigheaded... "Look around you. You can't take care of this yourself. You can't afford to hire someone. I'm offering my help in between my other jobs. What's the harm in that? I've been keeping an eye on your folks ever since I got back, Jazz. I'm not about to stop that just because you've blown into town with a stubborn streak a mile wide running down the middle of your back."

"Well, thanks for keeping an eye on them, but I've got it now. You can go live your life and forget all about us."

She was trying to rile him into a fight. Luke knew it and still took the bit in his mouth. Almost. Staring at her, watching the fire in her eyes, seeing the tinge of fear behind the fire, he did the only thing he could do. Right there on the slanted roof, he kissed her. Not the easy, gentle kisses he'd dreamed about. This one was hard and full of passion and pent-up emotion. From both of them. He held her shoulders, bracing her as his lips moved over her willing ones. She kissed him back just as hard. And with just as much passion, with her hands holding tight to his arms.

When he broke the kiss, he leaned his forehead against hers and spoke more quietly than the raging emotion he felt inside. "I'm not going anywhere."

Making sure she was steady on her feet, he let go, grabbed his tools, and climbed down the ladder. He marched back to his house without looking back.

~~~

Jasmin watched him walk off, fingers on lips that tingled with leftover need. The chill from his absence caused her to hug herself. She'd been furious with Luke for going ahead with the roof repairs when she'd told him not to. Then she'd let him kiss her? Worse, she'd kissed him back and liked it. A lot. What the hell had that been about?

Shaking her head as he disappeared into the brush that bordered their properties, she looked at the roof. Tar glistened all over the place, but it looked uniform and like it had a purpose. Not haphazardly thrown down with the hope that it would stop the leaks like she'd have done. She could also see at least five places where he'd replaced shingles. The man knew what he was doing and did his work well.

Damn it.

Jasmin climbed down off the roof and put the ladder away, then went to free the horses from the confinement of the trailer. By the time she'd cleaned the stalls, brushed and fed them all, and headed for the house, she was bone-tired.

As usual, her father sat on the porch smoking his pipe. Tonight, he had a glass of wine in his other hand. An envelope sat on the table next to him, but he picked it up and stuffed it in his pocket.

"How'd it go?" he asked.

"Fine. We rode down to the point where the family spread the ashes after saying a few words. It seemed good for them." She'd like the poem they'd read. Something about family and forgiveness being the most important things in life. It had struck a chord with her. After a month of grumbling around, she needed to stop taking her frustrations out on her mom and dad. They'd done their best and now it was up to her to help them keep their dream for as long as possible.

"Good. Need any help with the horses?"

She sat down and pulled off her boots, shaking her head. "No. They're brushed, fed, and bedded down. How was Mom today?"

Her father took a sip of wine and paused to look out over the yard before answering. "Argumentative."

"Ah, man, I'm sorry. Need me to run interference?"

"No. I finally gave in and helped her back to bed."

Jasmin bit her lip to keep her frustration from showing. "How long was she up?"

"Made it an hour."

Not long enough. With a sigh, Jasmin stood to go inside.

"I made dinner early and fed your mom. There's leftovers in the fridge for you."

"Thanks, Dad. I'm famished." She opened the screen door but stopped and turned back to him. "Hey, it's about winemaking time, right?"

"Yep. My friend said the grapes are on the way and should be here soon."

"Friend?"

"As long as I only make wine for friends and family, he's generous and gives me the grapes for free."

A cost Jasmin hadn't considered.

"Any chance you'd show me your process? Let me help?"

He regarded her for a long moment, as if he knew where she was going with this. "Sure," he finally said. "I'd like the company."

"Great. I'm going to eat and head to bed. Lots on the agenda, including winemaking." She smiled. "G'night."

"Good night, Jasmin. Sleep well."

Inside, she heated the chili and cornbread, set out salad, and ate almost without noticing. Working with her father making wine would give her more opportunity to consider how to go commercial with it. And to convince her father it was a good idea.

Her list of to-do's sat in the middle of the table. She grabbed a pen and wrote *make wine* toward the top, then scratched out *repair roof*.

The roof, the biggest issue on her make-it-or-break-it list, as she'd come to think of it, had been taken care of, or at least bumped to low priority until they could afford a new one. Thanks to Luke Taylor. And she'd been pretty mean to him about it. That bothered her, but Powters were proud.

They didn't take charity. That's how she'd been raised. She'd made her own way in the world, at least until recently.

Jasmin put her dishes in the sink and went to bed, too tired to think anything else through. Tomorrow was a new day with new problems, and she needed sleep to tackle them.

If only she could stop thinking about standing on a roof being kissed like she was the only woman on earth.

If only.

Chapter Five

Gladys, just starting her daily stroll about town, saw Luke's truck coming down the road and flagged him down.

"Hey, Miss Gladys. Do you need a ride?"

"Oh, no, dearie." She slapped legs that, despite all her walking, had begun to creak almost as bad as Mabel, her affectionately named shopping cart. But no need for anyone else to know that, at least not yet. "These legs still get me anywhere I need to go. I was just wondering if you were going to the Cannery Park opening ceremony on Saturday?"

"You know I am. I asked if you needed a ride and you turned me down."

"Ah, yes. You're just too good looking and you'd keep the others away."

Luke blushed, which she loved seeing. Such a shy boy.

"Well, have you found someone to escort?"

The blush turned into a deep scowl. "Nope."

"Really? Not even that nice Powter girl who's moved back home?"

"Definitely not her." Luke stared straight ahead, an emotionless mask replacing his scowl.

Something was up between those two. Something had gone wrong. Gladys was certain they were meant to be together, but love sure needed a lot of nudging these days.

"Well, then, I'd like to rethink my earlier refusal. Would you escort me to the opening?"

He turned toward her in slow motion, as if it was hard to give up what, or who, he'd been thinking about.

"I'd be honored to, Miss Gladys. I can pick you up."

"Oh, no, can't be seen in that neighborhood. Nosiree. You can pick me up at Bernie's pizza place. Two p.m. sharp."

Luke laughed. "You strike a hard bargain, but I'll be there."

"Thank you, dear."

Luke waved and headed out, leaving Gladys to watch his truck move down the road. "I won't be the only one waiting for you," she muttered as she ambled down the road, pushing her Mabel into the main part of Willow Bay.

"No, sir. I won't be the only one."

~~~

"I'm going into town for some groceries," Jasmin hollered as her dad walked past, leaning heavily on his cane.

"Don't forget your mother's peaches."

"I won't." Canned peaches from the grocery store, not the root cellar, had become the only thing that would put a smile on her mother's face these days.

Jasmin fired the truck up and let it idle as she watched her father head for his wine-making shed. So much for involving her. Jasmin couldn't help but smile and shake her head as she pulled out of the yard. That kind of stubbornness was the Powter legacy. Her father had done things his own way for so long, he probably didn't know any better. Like the time he decided to drive to Chehalis for a deal on some horse tack. In winter. With snow already falling inland. He'd gotten stuck there for three days. Jasmin's mother had a very low-voiced, don't-mess-with-me discussion with him when he returned. Her father was stubborn, but her mother had always ruled the house.

Before heading to the grocery store, Jasmin went down to the beach. She rarely got to enjoy a walk here. By the time she finished with horses and rides, she just wanted to go home.

Spying Luke's truck, Jasmin groaned and seriously considered turning around. No way did she want to rehash that episode on the roof. Her brain, heart, and every other part of her brought it up on too regular a basis already.

The man seemed to be everywhere. Today, he fished. Avoiding him—the smart thing for her to do—was damn near impossible. He turned and waved to her. Caught, Jasmin parked next to his truck. If she couldn't avoid him, she might as well join him. She'd just have to keep her distance. Being close to Luke Taylor was dangerous. If he'd left her once, he'd do it again. And Jasmin wasn't sure she'd survive a second time.

He cast into the surf, a solitary soul against the vastness of water. Luke had fished as long as Jasmin had known him, mostly with his dad by his side. Her parents had told her about the accident that had taken both Luke's parents from him. That must have devastated him.

She walked to the water's edge. The man must have eyes in the back of his head because he reeled in his line and joined her, his waders slapping the water with each step.

"Hi, Jazz." Wariness shadowed his eyes.

"Hey, Luke."

"So, you're speaking to me then?"

"Why wouldn't I?" *Please don't bring up that kiss. Please, please, please.*

"Because I dared to help you by repairing the roof."

Oh, thank God. Jasmin breathed a sigh of relief, then swallowed that breath as Luke's gaze dipped to her lips, then back up. Damn it. He knew exactly what she was thinking about.

"I—thank you, Luke. For the work on the roof, I mean."

"See, now that wasn't too hard to do, was it?"

Jasmin shook her head. "We need to be able to take care of ourselves, Luke. I can't always be calling on you to help out."

Luke closed the distance between them and Jasmin sidestepped. Together, they walked along the water's edge. "You can, you know. Call on me. Always."

Always? Or until he found the next reason to leave? "That's not fair to either one of us."

She glanced at him. She could tell he wanted to say more by the way he worked his jaw. When he did speak, his question caught her off guard. "Tell me about your life in New York."

"Really? Why do you want to hear about that?"

He shrugged, a guarded expression on his face. "It's where you've spent most of the years since we graduated. You were all hell-bent on getting there. I'm curious if it was everything you thought it would be."

If he had come with her like she'd wanted, he'd know, same as her. "It was awesome, Luke." Jasmin grabbed his arm. "Crazy and expensive and engines full throttle. I felt alive there. I think you would've liked it."

"Me? In the city that never sleeps? No thanks."

"Really?"

"I'm Willow Bay born and bred, Jazz. I don't care if I ever leave here. But I know you needed to go. You needed to spread your wings." He stopped her with a hand on her shoulder. "Did you find what you were looking for?"

The intensity of his gaze surprised her. This question, and her answer, were important to him, so she selected her words carefully. "I followed my passion, web design. I managed to work and go to night school and get my degree." That had been the culminating moment of her time in New York, when she'd gotten her degree. Though, looking around the audience as she walked across the stage to collect it, she'd seen no friendly faces. She hadn't told her parents until afterward because they couldn't afford to come out. Plus, she'd had to work the next day, and her parents never did understand her passion for "the internet." Still, the day had meant something to her.

"I wish I'd been there to see you get your diploma." He touched her cheek before dropping his hand. "You should be very proud of that."

Luke got her. Unlike her parents, he understood a passion like hers. Tears stung her eyes and Jasmin turned away to hide just how much his praise affected her. Sniffing quietly, she started back toward her truck. Luke turned with her.

"How were the Marines for you? Did you find yourself there?"

He didn't answer right away. When he did, the tone of his voice made Jasmin look at him. His face—a mask of stone—worried her. "The Marines were fine. The conflicts weren't. Hoo-rah."

Now Jasmin was the speechless one. She knew he'd gone overseas, but he'd never written a word in the sparse letters they'd exchanged about being deep in trouble.

Jasmin stopped and turned him to look at her. "Were you injured?" She looked him up and down, as if she might see gaping wounds straight off the battlefield.

"Not a single physical wound."

His monotone voice heightened her concern. Luke hadn't come home unscathed, if his tone was any indication. "Luke, are you okay?"

"I'm fine." He stuck out his jaw and resumed walking,

at a faster pace. Jasmin had to quick step it to catch up with him. They made it to their trucks without any more conversation. Jasmin leaned against hers as she watched Luke break down his pole and stow his gear.

"Thanks for the walk, Jazz. I'm glad you had a good time in New York."

He climbed in his truck like he was just going to leave. Jasmin knocked on the passenger window and Luke, looking like a dog about to go inside the vet's door, punched the button to lower it. "What?"

"If you, umm, ever need to talk, well, I'm here."

"Yeah, but for how long?" He stared at her, his eyes flat and emotionless, before he started the truck and pulled out, leaving Jasmin open-mouthed and in shock.

As she climbed into her vehicle, Jasmin remembered. She'd accused him of the exact same thing when he'd offered to fix the roof. A shot across the heart for both of them. Except he'd left first. She'd only left because he'd joined the Marines. Jasmin sighed, started her truck, and pulled out more slowly than Luke had. She headed for the grocery store, her heart hurting for Luke, for herself, for their eighteen-year-old selves.

After the grocery store, she stopped for pizza. She and her folks deserved a night off.

"Hey, Jasmin," said Bernie, the flame-haired owner of Square Peg, as she walked by with a yummy-smelling pizza. "I've hardly seen you since you got back to town."

"Hasn't been much time."

After Bernie set the pizza down in front of a couple Jasmin didn't recognize, she pulled Jasmin over to the counter and nudged her onto a bar stool. She slipped behind the counter and opened the fridge, glancing back at Jasmin. "Beer or wine?"

"Wine, definitely. Just the one, though. I've got to drive

and there's more work to be done."

"There's always work and we all need a break sometimes." She set a glass of red in front of Jasmin. "It's not your Dad's, but it'll do."

"Thanks. How are you feeling?"

Bernie rested a hand on her burgeoning belly. "I feel every hour of the day here, and I'm tired all the time. And in the bathroom." She laughed.

"You wouldn't change a thing, would you?"

"Nope. Not a single thing. How's your mother doing?"

Jasmin shook her head. "It's day-to-day."

"I'm sorry." Bernie patted her arm.

"I don't understand why she won't even try." Deep down, Jasmin also worried about whether she was doing the right thing, almost badgering her mother. Frustrated and confused about the way her mother had given up, it was hard to figure out the best thing to do.

Coming around the counter, Bernie flopped on the stool next to Jasmin. "You know, when I ended up out on my own, I copped the attitude that if I couldn't do it myself, I wasn't doing it."

A runaway, Bernie had lived on the street for several years before coming to Willow Bay, or so Jasmin had heard. "You sound like my mother. She's always been that way. She's always wanted to learn things herself. Until now."

"When someone realizes they can't do something without help, it's easy to want to give up. And Katherine can't do this alone. She needs help. That's probably rough on her."

"It's rough on us all, especially my dad. I just want her to get better. As much as she can." Jasmin hung her head, unsure why she'd opened up like this. She barely knew Bernie, having left town about the time Bernie showed up. "Sorry. I must have needed to unload."

Bernie gave her a hug. It felt so good, Jasmin hung onto her.

Stepping back, Bernie tucked Jasmin's hair behind her ears. "Honey, you come in here and unload any time you want."

Once Jasmin ordered her pizza, they chatted about Willow Bay while it cooked.

"Hey, you aren't looking for any help here, are you?" Jasmin asked.

"We're full up with help right now. Don't need much at the moment anyhow since the season's winding down. You looking for work?"

"Yes. We're done running horses, so I thought I'd try to find a job to help tide us over. Anything would do. I'm pretty much a jill-of-all-trades."

"I don't know of anyone hiring at the moment, but if I hear of anything, I'll let you know."

"Thank you. I appreciate it."

"Oh!" Bernie said, glancing outside. "There's Gladys. Let me check on her real quick." She disappeared out the door. Jasmin watched them chat. She'd only met Gladys a couple times but knew she was beloved by the entire town. A street person *and* a matriarch—an interesting mix.

A buzzer sounded in the back and Bernie whizzed by. "That's your pizza. I'll get it boxed for you."

A few minutes later, Jasmin left with a delicious-smelling pizza in her hands to find Gladys leaning up against the truck, her handy, tarp-covered shopping cart beside her.

"Just the person I wanted to speak to," Gladys said.

Jasmin grinned. It was hard not to when Gladys's face showed so much joy for life. "Hi," she said. "What's up?"

"Are you going to the Cannery Park opening on Saturday?"

"I don't think so. I have a lot of work to do." And the

idea of running into Luke, well, that was probably a larger part of her reason for staying away. He didn't need her interference any more than she needed his. Apparently.

"Dear, this is the event of the year for Willow Bay and it's been a long time coming. You have to go. Everyone will be there."

Exactly why Jasmin wanted to avoid it. "I don't know. I take care of my mother and she won't go out in public."

"I understand that. I suspect your father won't want to go, either. He sticks pretty close to Katherine, God bless him. But that's no reason for you to stay home. Come out, have some fun." Gladys leaned in. "I have it on good authority there will be samples of chowder there, advertising our first annual chowder festival coming up this winter." Gladys stood tall, obviously proud of what Willow Bay was accomplishing.

"Why are you asking, Gladys?"

"Well, because I'd like a ride and I think you and this old truck would be the perfect entrance for me. Not too flashy."

Willow Bay helped out its own. Jasmin needed to get behind that. Apparently, that meant she was going to the celebration on Saturday. "Sure, I can give you a ride," she told Gladys.

"Ahh, you are so sweet." Gladys patted Jasmin's cheeks. "If you could pick me up here at two p.m., that would be perfect."

With that discussion over, off Gladys went, heading who knew where. Jasmin drove home wondering how a street person had just bamboozled her into going to the park opening.

Chapter Six

Luke tugged on his bolo tie and ran a comb through hair that did what it wanted no matter how he tried to tame it. That's why he wore it short. Just easier. It would also be easier to skip this park opening. How he'd let Gladys talk him into going, he didn't know. Socializing wasn't his forte, not since he'd been overseas. Sleep-deprived yet again, an afternoon nap sounded better than this.

But he'd promised, so he pulled on his cleanest ball cap, grabbed his wallet and keys, and headed out the door, bracing himself to spend the afternoon with the masses. At least the weather was cooperating. The rain would hold off until tonight.

He pulled out of his driveway in time to see the Powter truck leaving. Had Jasmin and her father convinced Katherine to go to the opening? Pretty hard to believe. He'd tried to visit with Katherine several times and had been kindly refused by Ned, with apologies.

He only saw one person in the truck. Jasmin? Things were looking up if she'd be at the park opening, no matter that he shouldn't want to see her. She obviously didn't want to run into him. Luke followed her into town and down the main stretch until she pulled into the Square Peg parking lot.

And no Gladys anywhere that Luke could see. Confused, he pulled in and parked next to her. He got out, rounded his truck, and tapped on her window. Jasmin rolled the window down looking like she'd rather be anywhere than right here, right now. Even so, she was just about the most beautiful thing he'd ever seen. Curvy dark curls, down for a rare moment, framed a tanned face that didn't need enhancing, though she wore some makeup. Dangly golden earrings peeked out from beneath her hair and her normal t-shirt and denim shirt were gone, replaced by a long-sleeved dark-colored lacey number that looked good on her. Really good.

"Fancy meeting you here," he said.

"Yes. Fancy that," she said.

"Are you going to the Cannery Park celebration?"

Jasmin heaved a deep sigh. "Yes."

"You don't sound too excited."

"I sort of got talked into it."

Luke chuckled. "Me, too." He glanced around. Where was Gladys? "Why are you stopping here?"

"Gladys asked me to pick her up here." Jasmin looked around. "I wonder where she is? I sure hope she's all right."

The little meddler. With a not-so-well-hidden smile, Luke shook his head. "Oh, I'm sure she's just fine."

Jasmin looked at him, her squint filled to the brim with suspicion.

He held his hands up. "Not my fault, but I think the town meddler is up to her tricks again. She also asked me to pick her up."

Realization widened Jasmin's eyes. "She's trying to throw us together?"

"Looks that way." Not that he minded. Gladys and her matchmaking had totally brightened the day. He decided to embrace it.

"Then I'm going home."

"Why? You're dressed up. It's a great day for late September. Let's go enjoy the opening."

"Together?"

Ouch. Her voice, full of incredulity, knocked him down a peg. Luke put his arm on the open window frame and leaned closer. "Sure. Why not me?"

"Well, because— "

"Are you still mad at me for fixing your roof? You thanked me."

"Well, no, but— "

"But what? Jasmin, if nothing else, we're neighbors. We should be able to socialize, differences be damned. I'm not asking you to marry me. Just go celebrate with Willow Bay. Take the afternoon off from everything that makes you grumpy and laugh a little."

"Where everyone will see us and assume we"—she gripped the steering wheel tightly—"have something going on."

More and more, Luke wished for exactly that. It wasn't fair to Jasmin, but right now, he wanted nothing more than to spend the afternoon in her company.

"That would be horrible." Luke tried hard to look serious, but he couldn't pull it off. He straightened and grabbed the door handle.

"Got the guts?"

Jasmin scowled at him for dangling bait he knew she couldn't resist. The girl had always loved a good dare. He waited, giving her time to make her own decision, then almost whooped when she nodded.

"Great. I'll drive," Luke said.

She opened her mouth, then shut it and nodded again. Rolling up her window, she climbed out after Luke opened her door. He turned around and opened the passenger door of his truck and bowed. "Your chariot awaits, milady."

Her scowl deepened. "Just don't go getting any ideas about us," she said as she climbed in. "Because we"—she pointed between them—"are not happening."

We'll see about that. Luke's grin widened as he closed the truck door and went around to get in the driver's side. "You look very nice today." She did, with the long, flowing skirt and lacy tunic the same deep chocolate as her eyes. "Almost like you're trying to impress someone."

"I suppose I picked up that habit in New York. You know, looking decent when I go to events. Guess it's not a small-town thing."

With her scowl firmly in place, Luke couldn't help but chuckle as he pulled out of the parking lot and headed for Willow Bay's new park.

Yep. Today was looking up.

~~~

Today couldn't be going any worse. Jasmin stared out Luke's truck window as he brought them closer and closer to the celebration. All of Willow Bay would be there. The gossip mill would pair them up and Jasmin didn't want a relationship. Didn't need a relationship. Didn't have time for one. Especially not with the guy who deserted her after two weeks of the best sex she'd ever had. And damn it, she hadn't found that since, though she hadn't tried very hard. Why did Luke Taylor have this hold over her? And why now? In coming home, Jasmin seemed to have lost total control of her life.

Luke pulled into the lot across the street from the event and parked. Might as well get this over with. Jasmin reached for the handle.

"Wait." Luke turned toward her and touched her shoulder.

"What?" She couldn't quite look him in the eye, so she stared straight ahead.

"Can't we just enjoy today?"

"Being set up by Gladys and having everyone in town decide we're a couple?"

"You don't have to make that sound like a death sentence, you know."

"Kind of feels that way right now," Jasmin said.

"Ouch. I tell you what. Let's make a pact."

"Like we did that summer?"

"You know, we need to talk about that one of these days."

"No need to talk about it at all." Jasmin fidgeted in her seat and still couldn't bring herself to look Luke in the face. Did they have unresolved issues? Hell, yes. But did they need to dredge them up and go through that all over again? No. No. No.

"The fact that you keep bringing it up belies your statement."

How dare he. Jasmin opened her mouth, then froze without saying a word when he held up his pointer finger, a very effective shutdown. Damn it.

"Let me say again, I'm not asking you to marry me." He paused. "It's an afternoon, Jazz. No strings and more importantly, no work."

"You always have an agenda."

"Not today. Honestly, I just want you to relax and have one moment of fun. One afternoon. That's my only agenda."

Today.

"You didn't put Gladys up to this?"

"Hell, no. But once I realized her plan, I was all in. Seriously, though, if I have to walk six feet away from you, I will. I just want you to do something other than worry about roofs and horses and bills. A few hours, that's all this is."

Jasmin didn't like being coerced by anyone. While Luke seemed sincere about not being part of some larger plan to throw them together, the fact that he seemed to just want her to relax also seemed genuine. So what did she want to do? Go home, back to a mother fighting her at every turn, a father keeping wine secrets, and a house falling down around her? Or did she want to forget everything for a little while?

God, that would be so nice. To forget, to be free of all the worries. For a few hours. Was that worth a bit of gossip? Could she do this? Enjoy the day and not think about the baggage in her life? A grown woman now, she could keep this damn attraction for Luke under wraps. It's not like when she'd been a teenager. She knew the score now and had enough wisdom and guts to keep her wits about her. Right?

She glanced at Luke, who sat patiently waiting for her to think it through.

"All right," she said.

"Kind of sounds like you're heading for the gallows, but I'll take it." Luke grinned and threw open his door. He leaped out and grinned at her. "What are you waiting for?"

"A good reason to do this?"

"Relaxation. That's the best reason of all." He walked around the truck to open her door, laughing when Jasmin leaped out.

"All righty, then. Let's go have some fun."

Jasmin couldn't help but chuckle as she joined him. She reached for his hand without thinking, pulling back at the last moment. Friends. Nothing more. Except that sizzling rooftop kiss belied the whole friends thing. Luke's ability to rock her world hadn't changed on bit. Jasmin sighed.

Luke, a step ahead of her, turned back. "You all right?" Concern furrowed his brown.

"Luke, I can't go back. Not to what we were. I'm too frazzled right now to even think about it."

He reached up to tuck a loose strand of hair behind her ear. "Today isn't about that kiss."

Why did he always have to zero in on her thoughts so well?

"Let's just try to enjoy the day. That's all this is about."

Jasmin let her worry out, just for a moment, staring at Luke. "I wish I could." It would be so nice to just let go. Until some solutions were found, she couldn't think about anything else but keeping her parents safe and healthy. She looked up at a sky that got a little grayer. Perfect timing. Luke was right. Relaxing for an hour or two couldn't hurt, right? Jasmin put on her rusty game face and headed for the park at Luke's side.

Chapter Seven

Without much hope for a peaceful time between them, Luke escorted Jasmin through the entrance to the new park. The foundation of the old cannery was now a skate park, with basketball courts lining the front. The rest of the acreage was grass and pathways and gardens full of native plants. Bathrooms and lots of park benches—at the behest of Gladys—completed the look.

The change was nothing short of extraordinary. Luke would enjoy walking these paths once the crowds and celebrating were done with. There was an almost zen-like feeling about the place. He glanced at Jasmin to see her reaction to the spot's transformation from the overgrown, weed-encrusted mess it used to be.

He was shocked to see her smiling. Smiling! It transformed her. Jasmin had always been beautiful, but when her happiness showed, she took his breath away. She glowed with joy, something she deserved to feel every moment of every day. And, God help him, he wanted to be the one to give her that happiness.

"The park looks great, doesn't it?" Jasmin said, twirling around as she took it all in.

"It does." The sun shone on the new grass coming up

thick and green between the meandering pathways. Someone had even thought to put in two sandboxes, one for kids and full of beach toys, the other with a rack of rakes for contemplation. And on opposite sides of the park, too. Smart planners.

Luke was in heaven. Jasmin walked beside him as they wandered among the booths selling wares. She seemed happy for the first time since the broken saddle incident.

"Oooh, this is so beautiful." Jasmin picked up a handmade ceramic dolphin and turned it over, a frown touching her face before she covered it up.

"Do you like dolphins?" he asked.

Jasmin nodded. "Dolphins, whales, basically any sea mammal. Oooh, otters, too."

"Seals?"

"I'd like them more if they'd leave some fish for the rest of us."

"They are voracious, aren't they?"

"I'll say." They laughed as Jasmin placed the dolphin back on the table and slid her hand reverently along its surface.

Luke made note of the booth and made eye contact with the artist, who quietly picked up the dolphin and set it aside. Jasmin had moved on to the next booth. She swirled a beautiful African print around her shoulders.

"My color?" she asked him.

"Every color is your color," he said, tightening the fabric around her shoulders and pulling her close for a moment. "Do you know how beautiful you are?"

"Really? You think so?"

She smoothed the fabric and looked away, though not fast enough for Luke to miss the vulnerability in her eyes. Did she not know how beautiful she was? Her eyes were deep wells of emotion, yet they could dance with laughter at the drop of a hat. Her hair, curled and loose for the moment, moved or lay quiet based on her mood. Right now, he wanted to run his hands through the strands, to see if it was as silky to the touch as he remembered. And her body—lithe and ravishing at the same time. Everything about Jasmin sang to him.

"You take my breath away," he whispered.

Time slowed as he gazed into her bottomless dark eyes. He reached up and cupped her cheek, their surroundings forgotten, his eyes, his entire body, focused on lips he wanted to kiss. Needed to kiss. When her tongue snuck out to wet them, he leaned in. Friends be damned.

"Hey, you two lovebirds."

The voice seemed far away until a hand landed on Luke's shoulder. He reacted instinctively, tossed into the past where you trusted no one, grabbing the hand and whirling to pull the perpetrator's arm behind his back. The enemy combatant didn't fight, but morphed into the dead eyes of the woman—

"Damn, Luke," the man he held said, gasping. "Let go."

Luke did. Of course, he recognized Willow Bay's mayor, but couldn't quite shake the vision. Past, present, it was all one. He took a couple steps back, jostling the table of ceramics. He heard voices, mumbling. Then someone reached for his hand, pulled him away from the danger. Dark, concerned eyes. Gentle eyes. Jasmin. His lifeline and the only thought that had kept him sane while he'd been deployed.

"Are you all right?" Her voice, low with worry, cut through the thick vines of memory. Luke shook his head, clearing the last of the tangle. He was home, in Willow Bay. With Jasmin. Luke pulled her into his arms, needing the solace, the peace he felt with her as the rest of the waking nightmare drifted away.

"Ugh," Jasmin said. "A little hard, Luke."

"Oh, sorry." He let go and backed away from her. He'd hugged her too hard? If he did that, what else would he do when these fugues hit him?

"I-I have to go." Not waiting for an answer, he walked away, shifted to a jog, then an all-out run. Not to his truck. To the beach, to the lighthouse. Where he could think. Reason. Calm himself and try to figure out what to do. Because right now, he wasn't so sure he wouldn't hurt someone if he kept going on like this.

He might hurt Jasmin, and that absolutely could not happen.

~~~

Certain her jaw had hit the new asphalt walking path in Cannery Park, Jasmin watched as Luke sped away. What had just happened?

"You all right?" Josh asked Jasmin. He ran a hand through his short, sandy hair.

"I'm fine, Josh. Not so sure about Luke, though."

They watched as Luke disappeared around a corner. Josh's wife Dana stood beside him and she was sure her own eyes reflected the worry in both of theirs.

"Never had that happen before. Luke's so quiet and mild-mannered," Josh said, putting his shoulder through its paces. "I've been with him a lot, working on various projects. He's never once gotten angry or gone off the deep end like that."

"Are you sure you're all right?" Dana asked him. "Doc's here somewhere. Maybe we should have him take a look?"

"I'm fine. He didn't hurt me, just positioned me so I wasn't a threat."

"What started it?" Dana stuck her arm through her husband's elbow, the one opposite his tweaked shoulder.

"I tapped him on the shoulder. Guess he doesn't like

being surprised?"

"He was in the Marines, right? And served overseas?" Josh nodded.

"Maybe it was some sort of PTSD thing?"

Jasmin didn't know Josh or Dana all that well, given they were both transplants to Willow Bay. Perceptive of Dana, to have picked up on the PTSD thing. And probably spot-on in her assessment. Jasmin didn't like thinking about what Luke had seen over there. That a simple touch to the shoulder could send him over the edge like this, made Jasmin want to cry. Damn it. It wasn't fair to him, or to anyone, to come back hurting like this. If she'd known, she could have watched for it, tried to calm him before he went off the deep end.

"How long have you and Luke been dating?" Dana asked.

And there it was. The thing Jasmin had wanted to stay well away from. "We're not dating. Not at all."

"You went to high school together, I heard," Josh said.

"Yep. And that's the extent of our relationship. Until Gladys pulled the 'Can you give me a ride, dearie,' with both Luke and me, then did a disappearing act."

"Oh, ho," Josh said, laughing. "If she's set her sights on you two getting together, you might as well just give in. Gladys seems to be the resident Cupid and she relishes the nickname just a little too much."

Dana laughed with him. "I credit her with getting us together."

Bernie from Square Peg Pizza and her husband, Paul joined them. "Us, too," Bernie said. "Gladys definitely had a hand in it. And she nudged Jackson and Aimi together."

"The sheriff and the attorney?" Jasmin had met them both and didn't think either one of them would let anyone *nudge* them into anything.

"We've all fallen into that lady's web," Bernie said, laughing. "I for one, am grateful. So, we're going to go check out that pumpkin carving station. Paul's got mean skills with a carving knife. Anyone interested?"

"Ooh, I'll go with you," Dana said, pecking her husband on the cheek before she wandered off with Bernie and Paul.

"What are you going to do about Luke?" Josh asked, hanging back and walking with her to the edge of the park.

When had Luke become her problem? Despite this callous thought, she knew. The stark fear mixed with raging anger on his face had almost undone her. Whatever had damaged his psyche, Jasmin wanted to fix it. Luke deserved to be whole and happy, not some PTSD-ridden vet.

"I don't know," she said. "Take it one day at a time, I guess."

"Do you need a ride?"

"No. My car's at Bernie's and that's an easy walk." She could see Luke's truck still in the parking lot. "I might hang around for a while, see if he comes back."

"You know where he goes a lot to think, right?"

"The lighthouse?"

Josh nodded. "Call me if you need anything, including an intervention. I'm in. He's too good a person to have this happen to him."

"Will do." Jasmin went back and forth about going to the lighthouse, waiting here, or going home. In the end, she decided that to raid the sanctity of his thinking place wasn't a good idea, but she wasn't ready to go home. She had a lot to think through. Picking the avenue of least resistance, she headed for Luke's unlocked truck and climbed in. She'd wait for a while, to see if he'd come back so they could talk.

That was the only weapon she had against whatever was going on with him. Speaking of which… Grabbing her phone while she could access wifi in town, she spent the next hour researching PTSD and what help, if any, was available locally.

Information was power and she needed some at the moment.

Chapter Eight

Luke walked back to his truck like a convicted man stepping up to the noose. He'd probably alienated half of Willow Bay today with that display. He'd seen people watching as he raced off. And Josh... Josh was a friend and he'd manhandled him. Luke owed the man a huge apology.

Then there was Jasmin. He'd blown that. Now that she'd witnessed him come unhinged, no way she'd want anything to do with him. Shit. Maybe he should just leave town, start over. Even though he knew it wouldn't help—that his nightmares would follow him anywhere—Luke still considered the possibility. At least he wouldn't have to look at the condemnation on Jasmin's face. Hell, he'd probably never see her again after today, anyhow. If he did, she'd bolt before he got a good look. He'd destroyed the one thing that was becoming important to him. Again.

When he got back to his truck, he was shocked to see Jasmin asleep in the cab. A glance at his watch verified he'd been gone for hours. He'd assumed she'd get a ride back to her car. Or walk. It wasn't far. He'd never have left her here if he'd thought she'd be stranded. Hell, he shouldn't have left her at all. Luke opened the truck as quietly as possible, but even new trucks liked to creak and moan. Jasmin opened her eyes and sat up. Damn, she looked sexy, all sleepy and tousled.

"You waited?" he asked.

"You're my ride."

He hated the wary look in her eyes. Had he scared her that badly? "I won't hurt you."

"I know," she said without hesitation.

"How could you know?"

"I'm not sure. Instinct?"

"You shouldn't be here. You shouldn't trust me. I'm… broken."

"I want to help."

His mistakes. His burden. Luke got in, slammed the door, and shoved the key into the ignition. He turned it over. "You can't." Throwing the gearshift into drive, he roared out of the parking lot and down the street to Square Peg, where her car was the only one parked. The pizza place had closed for the day due to the celebration. He roared up beside her rig and slammed on the brakes, not sure why her offer of help made him angry. Deep down, though, he knew why. He was supposed to be the strong one and take care of her, not vice versa. It might be old-time thinking, but that's how he'd been raised.

"Can't we talk about this, Luke?"

"No. Damn it. No. This is my problem. My penance. You. Can't. Help. Me." He stared straight ahead, his hands so tight on the steering wheel he thought he might pull it off.

"Penance? What penance? Luke— "

"You were right. It was stupid to think we could— " He gnashed his jaw. "Look, just leave it be. Go home. Please."

Jasmin got out of the car, but she held the door for a long moment until he looked her way. The sadness in her eyes almost did him in.

"I'll go home, Luke. For now. But this isn't over, not by

a long shot." She shut the door much more quietly than he had. Luke, unable to bear being near her any longer, peeled out of the parking lot.

~~~

Jasmin watched Luke race off. The man was mired in some deep, dark hole of PTSD misery, and must be carrying a heavy burden of guilt if he thought he had to do penance.

"You okay?"

Jasmin turned at Bernie's question. "I'm not sure."

"He didn't hurt you, did he?"

"God no. Luke would never hurt me."

"You sure?"

"Yes," she answered definitively, and she believed it. Luke wouldn't hurt her.

"All right then. Want to come in and have a glass of wine?"

"Thanks, but I need to get home. I've left Mom and Dad too long already."

"All right, but I'm here anytime. Oh, and I haven't heard of any jobs yet, but I've got my ear to the ground. If something comes up, I'll call you."

Jasmin gave Bernie a hug. She'd left Willow Bay because she'd felt suffocated by everyone knowing everyone else's business. Now, that comforted her. Maybe she'd just needed some years to recognize what she had here.

With a wave goodbye, Jasmin got in her truck and drove home. After she parked, she walked through the barn to check on the horses. Her father met her at the door of the barn, breathless and without his cane, his face a study in agony.

"Thank God you're home!"

Jasmin reached to steady him as he swayed on his feet. "What's wrong, Dad?"

"It's your mother. She fell. I just found her and I can't

get her back into bed."

With her heart in her throat, Jasmin raced across the yard and into the house. "Mom? Mom?"

In her mother's bedroom, the wheelchair was canted on its side near the window and her mother lay on the far side of the bed, on the floor. There was barely any room to maneuver on that side.

Jasmin scooted in beside her mother, whose eyes were open. Silent tears wet her cheeks.

"Mom, it's okay. We'll get you taken care of. Are you hurt anywhere?"

Her mother moved her mouth, but no sound came out. Ah, damn. Jasmin's breath hitched as she tried to keep from crying. She reached for her phone to dial 911. Her mother tried to bat the phone away so Jasmin restrained her arm until she got the call made. Then she called Luke. There was no one else around who could help.

"I'll be right there," he said, then the line went dead.

Her father joined them, still out of breath, but Jasmin had to keep her focus on her mother. Her leg looked like it was cocked at a weird angle, so maybe she'd broken her hip. Feeling carefully along the back of her mother's head, she couldn't discern any blood.

"Did she hit her head?"

"I don't think so. I don't know," her father said just as Luke raced in.

"Dad, go show the paramedics where we are when they get here. And for God's sake, use your cane. We can't have you falling, too."

"What can I do?" Luke asked, breathless, scooting across the bed to see the situation.

"I'm not sure. I guess I thought, with your experience, you might have dealt with some injuries?"

"Nothing like this."

Jasmin placed a hand on her mother's chest. "Her heart's racing and she's crying, so I think she's in pain. She can't tell us."

Luke laid on the bed, getting as close to Katherine as he could. Jasmin hated the fear and pain in her mother's eyes. Luke focused completely on her mother, smoothing her hair, talking to her in soothing tones.

"Help is on the way. We'll get you fixed up in no time. Just hang in there." Whispers, really, but her mother listened. So did Jasmin, his voice was so compelling. When he began to sing one of her mother's favorite songs, tears slid down Jasmin's cheeks. How did he even know this song?

Commotion outside meant the paramedics had arrived. Jasmin squeezed her mom's hand and backed out of the way as they entered the room.

"Come on, Jazz. Let's get out of here and let them do their work." Luke put an arm around her shoulder and led her out of the room. Her father stood there wringing his hands.

"She fell, but we don't know when," Jasmin told a paramedic, her voice shaking. "She's had a stroke and has aphasia and left-sided paralysis." Good. Her voice was stronger that time. "Her insurance cards and allergies and medication list are on her dresser."

"Is she okay?" her father asked. "If anything happens to her— Is she going to be okay?"

Reluctantly, Jasmin left Luke's comforting arms to hug her father. "We don't know. They'll have to get her to the hospital before we'll have any idea."

Her father melted in her arms, almost sinking to the floor. Luke helped him to a chair and Jasmin squatted down in front of him. "Can you tell me what happened?"

"We had an argument. At least, as much of one as we can these days. I went to get her up in the chair. As usual, she didn't want to do it. So I tried to make her, and she hit me with her good arm. Over and over. I— I got mad." He watched as the paramedics brought in a backboard.

"So I said, 'Fine, stay in bed,' and left. I only went to sit on the porch and cool down. I wasn't out of the room more than five minutes when I heard a noise, came in and found her on the floor. I think she tried to get out of bed by herself."

"Ah, Dad, I'm so sorry."

"Ahem." A paramedic stood behind them. When he had their attention, he continued. "We've got her on the backboard and stabilized. We've given her something for the pain. Thank you for having her med list handy so we could check and give her something. We're going to transport her to the hospital now."

Jasmin's father stood up. "I want to go with her."

"You can ride in the cab, but not in the back."

"I'll drive Jasmin and meet you there," Luke said. Jasmin nodded.

The stretcher was brought in and her mother settled on it, backboard and all. Jasmin stroked her mother's hair and kissed her forehead. She looked much more comfortable, though so frail it was scary. "We'll see you at the hospital, Mom."

Her father leaned down to kiss his wife's forehead, brushing a hand along her cheek. "I'll be right there with you, my love." He straightened, but not enough. His stooped shoulders showed how worried he was. Within moments, the paramedics had loaded Katherine, Ned, and all the equipment in the ambulance and pulled out.

With a deep, shaky breath, Jasmin turned to go back into the house. "I need my wallet and phone."

"I'm going to go get my truck," Luke said. "Back in a minute."

~~~

At the hospital, Luke dropped Jasmin off and went to park. For a long moment, he sat there worrying about Katherine and thinking about how screwed up life was. He'd steeled himself to never see Jasmin again. To let her go. Within an hour of that decision, she'd needed his help and there'd been no question in his mind. He'd lit out for her house almost before disconnecting the call. Somehow, the powers that be had decided to throw them together and he didn't know what to do about it. With his emotions so volatile—made worse by the lack of sleep—being around him was dangerous. He didn't want to put Jasmin through that but he also couldn't leave her in her time of need. And, if he was honest, he wanted to be around her. Craved it.

Some cosmic tide of fate had brought them side-by-side. All he could do for now was roll with it and stay far away from her if the PTSD hit him again. Not if, when. Luke wouldn't be able to bear watching her fragile trust turn to fear.

He locked the truck and hoofed it to the emergency room to join Jasmin and her father.

"They won't let us go back with her yet," Jasmin said, a quaver in her voice.

"She's with the doctors," he said, wanting nothing more than to pull her into his arms and make everything better. Instead, he crossed his arms over his chest. "She's being taken care of."

Jasmin smiled weakly and went to sit by her father, reaching for his hand.

"Do you need anything?" Luke asked. "Water? Coffee? Have you had dinner?"

No response came from Jasmin's father.

"Dad? Have you eaten?"

"I was too upset to eat after we fought. And I don't

think I could eat now if I tried."

"I'll go get some food and drinks," Luke said. "If you don't want them, no harm. If you do, they'll be here." He could feel his anxiety growing, never a good thing with his issues. He needed action and this would help. He lit out of there quicker than he probably should have and stopped in the bathroom to splash water on his face. Staring at himself in the mirror, he wondered how he was ever going to get through this mess. His past had invaded his present and if he couldn't get it under control, he had no chance at a future.

In the cafeteria, he grabbed sandwiches, chips, bottles of water, and a couple coffees. He took his time returning to the waiting room. A man in scrubs stood talking to Jasmin and her father.

"Fracture right below the femoral head. With the stroke issues, she's not a candidate for hip replacement, but we'll pin it and that should get her up and about again. It's lucky it was her affected leg. If it had been the other one, she might never walk again."

Jasmin's father slumped back down in his chair, but Jasmin stood stiff and straight. Luke could see her mind working, prioritizing her questions. She'd be firing away pretty quickly, which made him smile.

"When is surgery?' she asked.

"They're prepping her now."

"Can we see her beforehand?"

"Certainly. I'll have a nurse come get you in a moment. We've given her more pain meds, so she might be very groggy."

"I assume she'll need rehab afterward."

"That always improves the outcome."

"I'll want to work with the rehab folks," Jasmin said. "It didn't go so well after her stroke. She can be a bit… stubborn."

The doctor smiled, probably a little wider than was necessary. Luke took a closer look at him. Dark hair, caring eyes. A little too handsome with a very white smile. When he reached for Jasmin's hand, Luke clenched his own, crushing the box of food before he remembered what he held and forced himself to relax.

"There will be plenty of time to go over the plan. Right now, let's get her through surgery."

Had Jasmin leaned forward? Toward the doctor? Luke took a step but stopped when she backed up. To cover his tracks, he moved to the table beside them and set the food and drinks down.

"Thank you, doctor."

"You're very welcome. Like I said, a nurse will be out in a few minutes to bring you back." With a handshake and a nod to Ned, the way-too-handsome doctor walked away.

Jasmin sank down beside her father, whose head was bowed. "Surgery," he said. "She needs surgery. Neither of us has ever had surgery. How will she do with the anesthesia?"

"We'll mention it to the nurse so they're aware. They'll be careful, I'm sure."

He looked up at his daughter, stark fear on his face. "I can't lose her, bug. I can't."

"Let's not think like that. It won't help us through these next few hours."

"Powter family?" A woman in scrubs called from the ER doorway.

"That's us," Jasmin said.

"You can see your mother for a moment now. She'll be going to surgery in about fifteen minutes."

Jasmin went to grab her jacket.

"Leave it," Luke said. "I'll stay here with it. Go see your mom."

With a look of gratitude, she put her arm through her

father's and followed the nurse.

Now, it was Luke's turn to sink into a chair, more exhausted from today's mental and emotional upheaval than he'd ever been after an offensive. Katherine meant a lot to him. She'd been the calm in his storm since he'd come home. Helping at their place had kept him sane when there wasn't enough work to keep him busy.

All alone in the ER waiting room, Luke raised his eyes to the ceiling, looking beyond, searching, praying that it wasn't yet Katherine's time. For Ned, for Jasmin, for Katherine, and for him.

Chapter Nine

Jasmin sat in the uncomfortable chair in the bright and airy room and watched the therapist working with her mother. Surgery had gone well and the stubborn had returned. Her mother refused to lift a leg, much less attempt to stand. Trying very hard to remember how close they'd come to losing her mother only a week earlier, Jasmin ratcheted down her impatience. The therapist—her name was Shirley— transferred her mother to the seat-height mat with zero help from the patient.

Once she'd managed to comfortably position her uncooperative charge, Shirley turned to Jasmin, who'd come to watch for the first time. The room was a picture of hustle and bustle as other physical therapists helped patients with their exercises. All the therapists had encouraging smiles. Some of the patients smiled too, and some concentrated. And then there was her stone-faced mother.

"As you can see, your mother still refuses to help with her healing in any way," Shirley said. "Was she like this at home?"

Jasmin glanced at her mother, who looked up at the ceiling, unmoving. "Mom, you want to answer that?"

No movement. Not even a blink. Damn it.

"Pretty much the same as home," Jasmin said. "Haven't figured out what will motivate her."

Shirley turned back to Jasmin's mother. "Katherine, we'll put your legs and arms through passive exercises for today, but you'll need to start trying. If you don't, the only option is a nursing home. Medicare won't cover rehab unless progress is made."

"No nursing home," Jasmin said forcibly. That earned a glance from her mother. "I'll carry her everywhere and feed her spoonful by spoonful before I'll put her in a home."

"I understand that," Shirley said. "Can you do that and your job?"

"My job is taking care of our home and my mother. I'll make it happen. I have to."

When a tear trickled down her mother's cheek, it broke Jasmin's heart. She reached over and patted her arm. "Don't worry, Mom. You may be too stubborn for your own good, but I'm stubborner." She grinned, trying to dispel the depression that had settled over them. If that's what they had to do, then that's what they had to do.

Once therapy was done, Jasmin took her mother back to her room, which she and her father had tried to brighten up with pictures and flowers. Patients were supposed to stay in their wheelchairs during the day, so when her mother pointed to the bed, Jasmin steeled herself for the look she was about to get.

"You know the rules here, Mom. Bedtime is after dinner."

When her mother visibly slumped in her chair, Jasmin sat down on the bed and pulled her close, reaching for both her hands. "You know I'm not trying to be mean to you, don't you?"

Her mother raised her head, her eyes so full of sadness it about split Jasmin in pieces. "I just want you to get better."

She got a small, sad head shake for the comment.

"At least as better as you can be, which is a lot better than you are right now. I guess you're just plain tired of fighting. I get that. But I'm not ready to let go and neither is Dad. We need you to fight."

Jasmin rubbed her mother's hands, which were still lovely, even if one of them didn't work very well. Katherine Powter had always had beautiful skin and, until the stroke, had never looked her age. Her hair was peppered with more gray than the burnished red Jasmin had grown up with. She'd loved brushing her mother's long hair. Still did, for that matter.

Standing up, she got the brush, moved her mother to where she could look out at the garden, and began brushing her hair, humming as she stroked. Then, she plaited the strands.

"You know Dad wants you to come home, right?" Her mother didn't respond, so Jasmin walked around to make sure she hadn't fallen asleep. She hadn't. Instead, she stared out the window without acknowledging her daughter or what she'd said, breaking Jasmin's heart all over again. With a sigh, Jasmin went back to plaiting. Taking a deep breath, she continued.

"I want you home, too, Mom More than anything in the world. You may think I have a lot on my hands with the property and the horses and the bills, and I do. But none of that matters without you there. Remember how we used to finish up our day, after all the rides were done, with lemonade out on the porch? I want that again. To come home a ride and see you there, waiting for me. And Mama, if you think you're too much work for me, you're wrong. Sure, right now it would be hard, but you can get stronger. That's all we need to get you home. Where you belong."

Jasmin tied off her mother's braid and pulled her around

so she could squat in front of her. The tears on her mother's face both saddened her and made her glad. "I know it's not the same," Jasmin said, reaching again for her mother's hands. "And it will never be. But that doesn't mean we can't all be happy. That you can't be happy. We just need you better enough to come home and we can all be a family again. I would be content if you would only try a little harder to get back there. I love you so much, Mama. I want you to come home. I need you to come home. I need you to at least try."

For the first time since the stroke, her mother reached for Jasmin with her good hand, pulling her in to hug. Tears dotted both their cheeks as Jasmin backed away. "I'll be here tomorrow, just like usual, Mama. Gotta go do some stuff around the property now. I love you."

Her mother held onto Jasmin's hand for a moment longer before letting go. Jasmin left with a much lighter heart than she'd come in with an hour earlier. Maybe, just maybe, there was some hope.

"Oof."

"Oh, I'm sorry," Jasmin said, so wrapped up in her own thoughts she ran right into someone in the hallway. She straightened to look into bright blue eyes that crinkled at the edges to match a smile.

"Luke!"

"Fancy meeting you here," he said, still holding on to her arm where he'd steadied her when they collided.

She hadn't seen him since the day of her mother's fall. The same day he'd basically told her there could be nothing between them. Ever since, she'd thought of him way too often. "What are you doing here? Do you know someone in rehab?"

"Yes. Your mother."

Oh. "You're visiting Mom?" That was a stupid question. Distracted by how good he smelled, Jasmin had trouble focusing.

"I'm visiting my friend who happens to be your mother, yes."

"That's really sweet of you, Luke."

"Not sweet. She's a great lady."

They stood close enough that Luke reached out and tugged the ponytail sticking out from Jasmin's ball cap.

"Want to go visit with me?"

Wouldn't that give her mother ideas? "No. I've been here for a while and need to get back to work."

"Have you found a job in town yet?"

"No. With the summer tourist season over, there's not much available around Willow Bay."

"You'll find something."

"Yep. Eventually." Would it be in time, though? Jasmin's shoulders drooped. Yesterday's mail had brought more surprising news and none of it good.

"What's wrong?"

"Nothing," she said too quickly.

"Something is, because all of a sudden you look like you bit into a lemon."

"Nothing I can't handle."

"You don't have to do everything alone, you know."

She raised her head and shoulders, standing straight. "Yes, actually, I do."

"I want to help."

"Thank you, Luke, but you made it clear you don't want to be part of anything I'm involved in. Besides, these are my parents. I'll take care of things from now on. Thank you so much for your help, and have a good visit with Mom."

Ever since she'd involved Luke with her mother's injury, Jasmin had been filled with guilt and regret. She'd used him. She knew that. She needed to turn him loose, for both their sakes. It hurt to be around him because she needed him on so many levels. Ordering herself not to cry, Jasmin walked past Luke and down the hall as quickly as she could. She needed out of there. Now.

~~~

Luke watched Jasmin hurry away with so many contradictory emotions racing through him, he could barely breathe. She didn't need him adding to her woes, but damn, it was hard to stay away from her. He'd made it an entire week, thrown himself into a couple jobs he'd picked up and worked so hard he did nothing when he got home but fall asleep, exhausted. Except that worked for only so long. He'd woken up and lay in bed staring at the ceiling on more nights than he cared to say. At least that meant the nightmares weren't as frequent.

The pile of trouble on Jasmin's plate seemed to have grown. Luke wasn't sure what new problem had cropped up, but something had her more worried than ever. Damn it. She should be free as a bird, laughing, loving life, not buried in problems.

But family was family. If Luke's parents were still around, he'd do whatever he could to help them, just like Jasmin. He wanted to tell her what a blessing that was, still having her parents.

But he couldn't. He had no right to be involved, to lead Jasmin on when he wasn't a fit partner for anything. Luke headed for her mother's room, wishing he could find a solution to the Powter's issues. Then maybe he could back away, let them live their lives, and not think of them—of her—every single moment of every single day.

In the room, Katherine sat in her wheelchair pressed against the wall. She was trying to push the wheel with her one good arm.

"Hey, Katherine," Luke said. "You doing okay there?"

She shook her head furiously and pointed to the door.

"Need me to push you somewhere?"

She nodded.

"Okay, then." This was the most animated Luke had seen Jasmin's mother. He backed the wheelchair up, turning it toward the door. When Katherine pointed, he pushed her out to the hall, then to the left, following her finger. Eventually, they made it to what must be the therapy room. Low mats and exercise equipment bordered the large room.

"Katherine," a lady said, joining them. "You don't have an appointment until this afternoon."

Katherine pointed to the mat.

"You want to work out now?"

A vehement head nod.

The therapist looked at Luke. "I'm Shirley, Katherine's physical therapist. Are you family?"

He shrugged. "Close as I can be."

"She hasn't wanted to work out since she got here."

"She's the one that made me bring her down here. I caught her trying to push herself, but she'd turned into a wall."

Luke could see tears in Katherine's eyes as she grasped the therapist's arm. Shirley squatted down in front of her. "You decided you want to get better, didn't you?"

Another head nod.

"All right, then. You need to increase your strength and balance, so we'll work out. Will you work with the speech therapist, too?"

Working her jaw muscles, Katherine uttered a soft "ya."

"Wow." Shirley looked up at Luke. "Not sure what turned this around, but I'm happy to see it. I can take her from here."

"Even though it's not her appointed time?"

"If Katherine Powter wants to work out, we're working out."

Luke laughed and squatted next to Katherine's chair. "Okay then. I'll leave you in Shirley's capable hands."

Katherine reached with her good hand and touched his face. Luke kissed her on her cheek, hugged her, and walked out, knowing that the change in Katherine's attitude would carry him through the day. He wanted to tell Jasmin but decided she'd appreciate it more if she just saw it when she returned. Still, it buoyed him and made the day a little brighter.

He headed out to do some finish work at a job in a much better mood than when he'd arrived.

Chapter Ten

"Dad, how could you not tell me this?" Jasmin held the letter out for him to see. If she hadn't gotten the mail yesterday and opened this without thinking, she might still not know.

Her father, looking smaller than ever in the porch rocker, his cane tucked in between his hip and the chair, shook his head. "I couldn't figure out how to."

"We're barely making ends meet, and now we have a $10,000 bank loan that's in arrears? They're threatening to take the property." Jasmin stopped, pulling back to look out over the yard, barn, and various sheds. Seeing them in their true light. Ramshackle, run-down, and in need of so much repair. Yet filled with a quiet beauty, a feeling that could only be evoked by a happy childhood. She'd loved growing up here. And, until this moment, Jasmin hadn't realized she didn't want to give this place up. She wanted to be here. This was her home. She'd come back for her parents. Now, she would stay for all of them, including herself.

If she could climb this new hill, a debt that had just been thrust in her face. Her father sat quietly, shoulders bowed, as if waiting for a sentence to be handed down. Jasmin reached for her father's hand.

"Sorry I snapped. We'll figure this out."

"I'm sorry I let things get so bad."

"You were focused on Mom and doing the best you could."

"It wasn't enough."

"Try not to worry. I'll go talk to the bank and see if there's anything we can do."

He shook his head, misery written all over his face. "I've already done that and they gave us a continuance of six months. We're at the end of that."

Her face taut, Jasmin had to work hard to keep her voice calm. If she'd only known about this months ago. But, would she have come home? Her New York life had been in full swing and she'd loved it. Designing websites might not seem like something to be passionate about, but she was. And she was good at it. Getting that promotion, she'd been at the top of her game with nowhere to go but up. She might not have given moving home a second's thought and would have handled what she could from there. She might even have convinced her parents to sell the place.

She would never have realized how much she loves their property and would never have had her epiphany. That in itself would have been a huge personal loss. Unfortunately, her realization meant nothing to a bank. She needed a plan before it opened on Monday. Today was Saturday, which didn't give her much time to figure this all out.

Jasmin patted her father's hand. "We'll think of something," she said, but she wasn't so sure. She left to wander their property, hoping it would help her come up with some ideas. She started in the barn. Maybe they could sell some tack. Except, as she looked around the tack room, she realized everything was in about as sad a shape as her broken saddle. They had ten horses left. Any less than that and they wouldn't have enough to run the business.

She mucked out the stalls then herded the horses in. Once they were fed and watered, she settled them in for the night. Could she find a job at another stable? The closest one was an hour away, though. Maybe they could board horses here. She looked at all the empty stalls. Yes, they could board horses. Jasmin made a mental note to put the word out first thing tomorrow. And she'd need to do some research on prices tonight, though researching on a cell phone wasn't optimal. She'd reduced her cell phone plan to the lowest available and didn't have unlimited gigs for research. She'd tried to attach to Luke's wifi but he just wasn't close enough.

Leaving the barn, she wandered through all the outbuildings. None of them would really work for paid storage. Maybe they could store RVs and trailers. They had a large field behind the outbuildings. That might work. Another thing to get the word out about. Except none of that would be a quick fix.

Her father headed into his wine-making shack. Jasmin wished she could convince him to go commercial with that. It could bring in the income they needed. What else could they do? Her work-from-home web design idea had been put on hold because they couldn't afford wifi. But she could work at the library during the winter months, get her own website freshened up, and search for some work to get her portfolio in shape. She'd do that tomorrow, too.

So far, she'd had zero luck finding a job in town. Willow Bay might be heading into sleep mode for the winter months, but some things still operated. She'd make the rounds. Again.

Back in the house, Jasmin paced out her worry. She missed her mother and hoped she'd be able to bring her home soon. Standing in the doorway to the bedroom, she realized how dark and dreary it looked. Since it was too late to go back into town today, maybe sprucing up Mom's room would help Jasmin think.

Starting with the closet, she wrinkled her nose at the dust as she dove into the ceiling-high pile of clothes and junk. Everything came out until the bed was covered. She added garage sale to her mental list of ways to make money. At the very back of the closet, Jasmin found a large portfolio. Opening it, she was amazed to find professional-level photographs. Color and black and whites of the beach or horses or both. In summer, in winter, all the moods of Mother Nature showed in the pictures. Thirty of them. Where had these come from?

"Your mother took those," her father said from behind her.

Jasmin, eyes wide with wonder, turned to him. "She did?"

Nodding, he picked up the top one. "This was always my favorite."

"I've never seen these. They should be up on our walls."

"Your mother never thought they were good enough for display. She's always been too much of a perfectionist, I think."

"These are amazing." And right then, an idea began to form in Jasmin's mind. She closed the portfolio case and set it aside. Until she could talk to her mother, there was no sense sharing her idea and getting anyone's hopes up.

"Spring cleaning?" her father asked, looking at the pile on the bed.

"Yep. I needed a distraction and I thought sprucing up the room would be good for when Mom comes home."

"I like that idea. Maybe it will motivate her."

"I like the idea, too," Luke said from the doorway. "Can I help?"

"Better than I can," her father said, holding up his cane. "I'm going to leave this to you youngsters." He hobbled off and suddenly, the room seemed awfully small with just

Jasmin and Luke there.

"So, how can I help?"

"For a man who said we should stay away from each other, you sure show up a lot."

At least he had the grace to look sheepish. "Yeah, well, you're a hard person to stay away from."

She should send him packing. Luke was right that they should probably steer clear of each other. Jasmin needed her focus to be on home and finding a way to make money, not on how giddy she felt with this man in the vicinity. But she could use some help.

"Got any paint?"

"I can find some. A lighter color?"

"Yes. I'd like to brighten this room for Mom."

"All right. I'll go hunt up some supplies."

"And I'll deal with all the stuff I piled on the bed."

Luke peeked inside the empty closet. "Just throw a sheet over it. We'll put the bed in the middle and paint around it. That way, we can do the closet, too. And we'll have to put primer on. This paneling is too dark to skip it."

"All right. I think I saw some painter's tape in the junk drawer. I'll start taping."

~~~

In less than an hour, Luke was attacking the walls with light sandpaper while Jasmin, being more petite, painted the closet. Though he spent more time watching her move than actually working. In the tight space, Jasmin wiggled and wormed her way in and out of the doorway. Damn, but she had one fine ass. Luke grabbed his jeans, repositioning himself as she got down on her hands and knees. She'd clearly finished the overhead work.

She scooted in deeper, then backed out. Luke stood there, sandpaper in hand and jaw tapping the floor as she maneuvered through his imagination. Damn, damn, damn.

When she sat back on her haunches to inspect her work, he quickly turned back to the wall, attacking it with more zeal than a light sanding required. He thought about her mother, about jobs coming up, anything to take his mind off the vision of her and what he wanted to do with her.

He was so screwed.

"You haven't gotten very far."

Luke whipped around to find Jasmin standing nearby. Too near, too soon after the thoughts coursing through his body had settled in low and needy places. Luke shook his head, trying to clear his erotic visions. Of them. Together.

When he finally took a good look at her, he laughed, unable to help himself.

"What's so damn funny?" Jasmin said, hands on her hips.

That only made him laugh harder.

Under her glare, he tried to stifle his amusement. He really tried hard. Finally, he managed to squeak out a few words between guffaws. "You. White. Head. Toe."

"What?" Jasmin held her arms out and looked down at herself, almost swiping Luke with her brush. "Oh, my God!"

Her ponytail looked as if she'd backed into a wet, white wall. The rest of her usually dark hair was salted with white dots. A lot of white dots. Splotches of white dotted her face, her neck, and her t-shirt and sweats were whiter than they were gray.

"You look like you just got snowed on. Like, blizzard snow," he said, still unable to wipe the grin off his face or the laughter from his voice.

Jasmin stomped around the bed and pulled the sheet off the free-standing, full-length mirror. "Oh, my God. You're right. I'm covered in paint!" She stared at herself, then turned to Luke.

For one tense moment, he thought she might tip the

scale to anger. Her lips quivered.

Was she about to cry? Luke headed for her, ready to calm the upset. When she let out a very un-ladylike guffaw, he froze.

Her laughter rolled over him like a slow-moving sluice of warm water, the sound filling him with a peace that could quiet even the worst nightmares. Her mirth was contagious and he joined her in hearty laughter as he closed the distance between them.

"Did you manage to get any on the walls?" he asked, lifting the now stiff ponytail for a moment.

"I sure hope so."

They both looked in the closet, coated with the same paint that speckled Jasmin.

Luke sized up the job with his contractor's eye. "Actually, despite the paint all over you, you did a really good job here. It won't need a second coat."

"Neither will I," Jasmin said. She might be jesting, but Luke heard the pride in her voice. She was happy. At least for the moment.

"Even your eyelashes have paint on them," Luke said, cupping her chin and turning her to face him as he took a closer look.

Jasmin's quick intake of breath drew his attention to her lips, full, slightly parted, just begging to be kissed. He gazed into eyes that no longer sparkled with laughter but smoldered with remembered desire. Drawn beyond their differences, he accepted the invitation, kissing her with gentle regard. He wanted to deepen it, wanted to go so much further as his heart swelled with emotion.

But he didn't want to scare her away. Or pull her into his pile-of-shit life. So he kept it light. Swift. Too swift. To pull back was like fighting a force field. To make matters worse, Jasmin moved with him, keeping them close.

Luke ran his hands down her neck, her arms, and backed up enough to take her hands in his.

"I don't think either of us is ready to take this any further, Jazz."

His quiet words got through to her and she kept still. Her fingers touched her lips for a long moment before she looked up at him. "I'm not sure either of us ever will be," she said, regret hanging heavy on her voice.

A part of him had prayed for her to refute his statement, to grab hold of him, kiss him again, tossing care to the wind. But he'd said the logical thing and she'd responded in kind. There was nothing more to be done. For now.

He nodded. "What say we pound out the rest of this room then? Not sure about you, but I could use the distraction."

Her eyes dipped to his very tight jeans, then back to his face. "Good idea," she mumbled, then reached out to dab a large blotch of paint square in the middle of his t-shirt.

"The walls, missy. Put the paint on the walls!" he said, a smile cooling the fire in his veins.

"Oh. Is that where it goes?" Jasmin batted her white-speckled eyelashes at him and Luke damn near pulled her back into his arms.

She must have noticed, because she pointed behind her. "I'll take this wall." She backed away.

"Chicken," he muttered under his breath.

"Where you are concerned, Lucas Taylor, I am," she said quietly, then dipped her brush in the paint and swiped it across the paneling.

In some ways, so am I. Luke watched her for a moment more, then grabbed the roller, dipped it in the paint pan, and got to work.

Chapter Eleven

"We've been trying to resolve this with your father for months."

"But I only found out about this two days ago."

The bank manager, whose wife had been Jasmin's high school algebra teacher, ran a hand through his graying hair. He was just as frustrated as Jasmin. She knew that, but it didn't help.

"Don, please, I need a little more time to sort this out." Damn. Jasmin hated begging.

He sat back in his comfy leather office chair, taking a moment to stare out the window at the light rain. When he turned back to Jasmin and let out a big sigh, she held her breath.

"Did you know that Time Bank bought us out last year?"

"No, I didn't." Where was he going with this?

"We're not just a friendly local bank in a small town anymore. We're part of a bigger system and, as such, we have rules to follow."

Shoot. Jasmin slumped in her chair on the other side of his desk. "So your hands are tied."

"Pretty much. I was already pushing it by giving your

father the extra time." He took a second deep breath. "I've known your folks my whole life. Used to ride their horses when I was a kid." He leaned forward, placing his elbows on the desk. "If I give you thirty days, can you come up with a plan to catch up?"

Nodding effusively, Jasmin wanted to jump for joy. "Yes. Definitely. I can totally do that."

"And,"—he pointed a finger at her—"we'll need a significant down payment on the past-due amount by the end of that thirty days."

Jasmin gulped. "How significant?"

"Forty percent."

"That's four thousand dollars."

"Plus interest, so closer to four thousand. They haven't paid anything on the loan."

Where would she come up with that kind of money? Jasmin sank back into the chair.

"I'm sorry, but it's the best I can do."

She stood up. "I get it. I know you're being generous. Thank you for that. I'll figure it out."

"How?" he asked.

"At the moment, I'm not completely certain. But I have some irons I can toss into the fire." She shook his hand. "Thank you, Don. I'll keep you apprised of how things are going."

"I'd appreciate that. I'm going out on a limb for you and your folks."

"I know. I'm more grateful than I can say."

Jasmin walked out of the bank both hopeful and more depressed than ever. How was she going to come up with four thousand dollars in thirty days? She'd blown through what little she'd had in savings since she'd moved back here, keeping the place afloat. She stopped beside her truck, trying to think it through.

Figuring she had to start somewhere, she pulled her hoodie up against the rain, grabbed her laptop bag, and walked the six-block to the library, a better idea than wasting precious gas. Time to get some feelers out. She'd print the horse-boarding flyers she'd done up and distribute them around town. She'd revamp her website and search for some free web-design promotion sites to get the word out.

Then she'd go visit her mother. Whether she wanted it or not, it was time for some hard talk. About those beautiful photographs and the money they might bring in, about the garage sale Jasmin intended to pull together for next weekend. If Jasmin got no answers from her mother today, she'd have to take that as permission to do what she needed to do.

She had no choice.

~~~

"Jasmin," Luke called from about a block away.

With the breeze, he guessed she hadn't heard him. He thought he'd catch up to her while she stood beside her truck, but instead of getting in, she took off walking at a fast clip. Like she was on a mission. Luke didn't try to stop her. Instead, he headed into the bank to deposit some checks.

"Hey, Luke." A man headed Luke's way, One he knew, of course. Like Jasmin, he'd grown up with the people of this town and thankfully, called most of them friends. "Hi, Don. How's that granddaughter of yours?"

"Two already. Can you believe that?" Grabbing his phone, he pulled up a picture of a tow-headed, blue-eyed darling.

"Wow. She's cute. And growing up fast." Luke glanced outside at Jasmin's truck, then turned back to Don. "Was that Jasmin Powter who just left?"

Don's grin slid and worry flickered in his eyes. "Yes."

"Everything okay?"

"I can't divulge private information, Luke. Sorry."

He didn't need to divulge anything. His face told the story. The Powters were in dire financial straits and Luke would bet his time at the lighthouse that Don had given them as much leeway as he could. Damn.

"I get it. No worries."

Luke finished his business, pulled his ball cap tighter on his head, and walked out of the bank into the rain. Jasmin's truck was still there. He stared down the block, willing her to appear so they could talk. The sidewalk was empty. Plus, the rain had picked up. With one last glimpse down the street, Luke jogged to his truck and headed for home.

Probably for the better anyhow. With Jasmin's almost impenetrable pride-wall, he needed to think through what he wanted to say. He wanted to help her. Correction. He would help her and her parents. Somehow. He just needed to get her to accept the help.

~~~

Jasmin felt like a drowned rat. She'd updated her website and walked all over Willow Bay in the rain posting horse-boarding and web-design flyers. And God Bless this town, because no one turned her flyers down. A couple folks even knew people who might want to board their animals. Dana had told her she'd talk to Josh that evening about a website for Tangerine Treasures, her gift shop. She'd been hoping they could branch into online sales.

After she drove home and changed, Jasmin headed to the rehab facility to see her mother, though she probably shouldn't have. The rain was coming down in buckets.

Inside the center, she took a moment to steel herself against her mother's disinterest in, well, everything. Turning the corner into her mother's room, Jasmin found it empty. She checked the dining room and the television room for her mother's wheelchair with no luck.

Wandering the hallways, she happened past the therapy room and jerked her head in that direction when she saw something in her peripheral vision. "Well, I'll be damned."

Her mother stood—stood!—between the parallel bars. Jasmin froze outside the window, afraid to move, worried she would distract her mother.

"You've got this," Shirley said, standing in front of Katherine. "Pretend that's a cane your right hand is holding on to. Cane and affected leg move at the same time, then the stronger leg follows.

Her mother wore a plastic brace on her paralyzed foot and ankle that kept the foot flexed. Jasmin's eyes widened and she smothered a gasp with her hand as her mother leaned on the railing and stepped with her good leg, then dragged her bum leg forward.

Jasmin couldn't stand waiting outside a second longer. With tears stinging her eyes, she walked into the room. Her mother looked up, smiled, then faltered. Jasmin leaped forward, but Shirley was there, right beside her patient to offer support.

"Well," Shirley said. "We just learned that distractions aren't great when you're walking, at least not at this juncture. Hi, Jasmin," she said as if nothing out of the ordinary was happening.

"Hi, Shirley," Jasmin said, taking the unspoken tip from the therapist. "Hi, Mom. It's good to see you up. Really good." She kept her voice well-modulated and tried not to screech her happiness.

"I think you've got a couple more steps in you before we call it a day, Katherine. What do you think?"

Eyes shining with pride, her mother said "Yes" with barely a lisp.

Will wonders never cease? Jasmin, feeling a little weak in the knees, sat on a nearby mat and watched as her mother took four—four—more steps before one of the aides brought her wheelchair. The whoomph when she sat down made everyone laugh.

"You've earned a break for the rest of the day, Katherine." Shirley turned to Jasmin. "Normally, I'd ask her to wheel herself back to the room, but maybe today, we can let family take care of that."

Her mother shook her head and pointed to the wheels on her chair.

"All right, all right. The queen has spoken." Shirley released the brake and stepped back, hands in the air. "It's all yours, Champ."

Grabbing the wheel well, her mother pushed, correcting her direction with her good leg. It took a long time for her to navigate the hallway to her room, but Jasmin didn't mind one bit. Her mind whirled. What had happened to turn her mother around?

Once she reached the window in her room, her mother turned the chair so she could see her daughter. Tears streamed down both their faces. Jasmin rushed forward, got down on her knees, and hugged her mother long and hard. When she finally pulled back, her mother smoothed away the tears on her cheek.

"How— Why— Ah, heck, I don't even care. I'm just crazy happy to see you working on getting better, Mom. So blooming happy."

Her mother's lopsided grin widened. She pointed at Jasmin. "You."

"Me? Me what?"

"You. Talk."

Jasmin took a moment to process the jumbled sounds. "You mean when I was here the other day?"

She nodded. "Ne'er. Hur'. You."

"Mom, you could never hurt me."

"Shtop. Try. Hur'."

What had she said that turned her mother's attitude around? Jasmin didn't even remember, but she was overwhelmed. "I'm so grateful to see you working at getting better."

"Wan' go home." Her mother cupped Jasmin's cheek.

"And you will. Just as soon as you get a little bit stronger. Dad and I will bring you home. Oh, by the way, I painted your room."

The lopsided smile returned.

"I'm sorry I wasn't more supportive when I first came home," Jasmin said. "I think I needed to remember why I love it here. And that's coming along. But I promise, Mom, as long as you try, I'll try." Jasmin clutched her mother's hands, one paralyzed and unmoving, the other tightening its hold on her own hand. "We'll do this together, okay?"

Her mother nodded. Once. Emphatically.

The remainder of Jasmin's visit was full of smiles and love. She never brought up her mother's photography, unwilling to rock the boat in any way. In fact, even the incessant rain couldn't dampen Jasmin's spirits. When she got home, she saw her dad sitting in his usual spot. Good thing the porch was covered.

Pulling her jacket over her head, Jasmin raced to join him and get out of the rain. She shook off her coat and hung it under the eaves to dry. Crouching down in front of her dad, she rested her hands on his. His eyes were alight with joy and happiness.

"You knew!"

Ned Powter nodded, bringing Jasmin's hands together in a clap. "Your mother wanted to surprise you."

"The difference in her is amazing. It's just so hard to believe."

Tears formed in her father's eyes. "I don't know what

you said to her, but I'm so grateful you got through."

"Honestly, I'm not sure, either. But I need to get back to that bedroom of hers. We need to get it ready for her to come home!"

Jasmin worked late into the night, sorting clothes and putting the bedroom back together. She went up to the attic to look for picture frames and found several, but not without stepping around some wood tenderized by water leaks. All old, though, thank goodness. Jasmin sent a prayer of thanks Luke's way. He'd done a good job on the roof. Then she remembered weather even worse than today's soaking was on the way, and she felt more grateful to him than ever. A lump of remorse stuck in Jasmin's throat and she swallowed to clear it. Harsh didn't even begin to describe how she'd treated Luke. She really should apologize. Bury her stubbornness for once. He was a good man.

Back downstairs, she cleaned the frames and put some of her mother's photos in them.

"Sure looks nice in here."

Her father stood in the doorway. Jasmin grinned at him. "It's lighter and happier, don't you think?"

He nodded, the wrinkles in his own worn face easing with the smile he gave her. "You did a good thing here."

"And it didn't cost anything, thank goodness." Jasmin wanted to kick herself for saying that when her father's face fell. She went over and hugged him. "Try not to worry. I talked to Don at the bank and we've got another thirty days."

"To do what?"

"Give him a plan and a hefty portion of the arrears."

"How are we going to do that?"

Jasmin sat on her mother's bed. "I've put some feelers out to board horses, and I've got a couple other irons in the fire."

"Those don't sound like thirty-day fixes."

"They aren't, but they're part of the plan. Also, I want to hold a big garage sale, maybe make some money off some of this juh— um, stuff we've got around here. Things we don't use anymore."

"Oh, I don't know about that."

"Dad, you can have final say over what goes, but I'm going to start sorting and figuring things out. It won't help with the banknote, but maybe we can make enough to repair some of the tack, like my broken saddle."

"I guess we'll see what you come up with and go from there."

Jasmin would take that as a win.

"I'm off to watch a little television. Want to join me?" her father said.

"I want to finish in here. Enjoy."

As he smiled and shuffled away, Jasmin felt the weight settle on her shoulders again. Then she looked around the bedroom, at how fresh and new it looked. The beginning of another chapter in their lives. They'd find a way out of this somehow or another. They had no choice.

Chapter Twelve

The next morning, Luke climbed the stairs to the lighthouse to check that everything was battened down for the storm due to roll in later that day. This would be the first significant storm of the season and it was looking like a doozie. He went out onto the walkway to watch the sky roil and race, the wind shouting at him to go back inside. Gray clouds mixed with white ones for now, but the charcoal of a winter storm coming in early sat off in the distance waiting for the right moment to pounce.

"Hello?"

Jasmin? Luke looked down and saw her standing beside the lighthouse.

"Come on up," he hollered.

"What?"

"Come on— " Luke motioned with his arm for her to join him. Jasmin waved and disappeared. He went inside the round room that housed the light and waited while she climbed the four flights of stairs. Why was she here? Jasmin never sought him out, so this was either good news or she had another bone to pick with him. He took a deep breath to still his anxiety. He didn't need another episode. Not now. Not ever.

"Whew," she said, finally making it to the top level. "I can see why you're in such good shape."

Luke cocked an eyebrow. "Thank you."

When Jasmin blushed, she didn't do it half-heartedly. Her face, infused with red, was about the cutest thing he'd ever seen.

"You know what I mean," she said, not dodging because she'd blushed but standing proud.

"I do know what you mean. And might I return the compliment? You're looking especially lovely today, Jasmin. Like a breath of fresh air." With much trouble, he looked up from her form-fitting jeans to appreciate the fact that she didn't have her usual t-shirt on today. She wore a long-sleeved sweater that clung in all the right places. Places he wanted to cling to as well. Her hair was down, also unusual these days. Luke squinted. Was she wearing makeup? Jasmin didn't need makeup. She was beautiful in her natural state.

"Anything looks good next to the weather stirring outside."

Reaching for a lock of her hair, Luke ran the dark silken strands through his fingers. "Don't belittle yourself like that. You're beautiful, Jazz. You should own it."

This time, she turned away as the red colored her face. "You're biased."

"Completely and utterly," he agreed. He meant it. Luke was falling hard and didn't have the right to involve her in his problems. So he stepped back, taking the situation down a notch.

"How well do you know Gladys?" Jasmin asked.

Way better than anyone else in town, but he couldn't say that. "I see her around. Why?"

"I keep thinking about her setting us up the other day. Dana said she's the town matchmaker. Do you think that's true?"

Luke tried to chuckle but it got stuck in his throat. He hadn't thought about it until now, but Gladys had tried to throw them together. She'd helped others in Willow Bay break through their barriers to find love. Was she trying that with them? If so, he'd have to talk to her, and soon. Jasmin deserved better than him and his problems. "I'm not sure," he finally answered. "Gladys has a sharp mind and when she sets her sights on something, she's pretty determined."

Jasmin nodded and turned to look out the window.

"Let me show you my favorite place." He held out his hand. She took it and followed him out onto the walk.

Almost immediately, Jasmin's hair flew in all directions. The wind whipped around the lighthouse, then turned back on itself, creating a whirlwind.

"Whew," she hollered to be heard over the wind. "So this is your favorite place?"

Rather than yell, Luke leaned in to whisper in her ear, sorely tempted to nibble while he was there. She smelled so good. "Not normally this windy. Look at that view, though."

She did, and her mouth opened wide in an "oh" of astonishment. "It's beautiful. Mother Nature's majesty."

Luke agreed completely. Even with darkness rolling in, there was a beauty to the turmoil in the waves as they pushed treasures onto the beach and pulled sand back into the water.

Jasmin leaned into him, holding her hair against her head to tame the wind-tossed strands. "I get why you love it here, but can we go back inside now?"

With a laugh, Luke helped her through the door. The wind fell off as soon as he closed it. Jasmin tried to finger comb her tangled strands, but quickly gave it up as futile.

"Look what you did to me," she said.

"That's nothing compared to what you do to me," Luke tossed back quickly, berating himself as soon as the words left his mouth. Why did he keep saying this shit?

He wanted to take it back, but he would be lying. Besides, it was too late, if the round, serious look in Jasmin's eyes was any indication.

To hell with it.

He closed the distance between them and covered her mouth with his. No gentle reckoning this time. He wanted her bad and needed her to know that. When she sighed, he dipped his tongue past her lips. Then he waited.

When their tongues met and she accepted his offering, he drew her in tight to his body, craving everything she had to offer. They swayed back and forth. Luke gave himself over to the thrum, the lust that hardened him. Her lips were soft and inviting. At the same time, she demanded more, nipping his lower lip.

Luke wrapped his hand around the back of her neck, pulling her closer, loving her with everything he had to give.

Crack!

Luke and Jasmin flew apart as lightning lit up the lamp room. He counted silently. One, one thousand, two, one thousand, three—

Thunder rolled through in waves, rumbling in the lighthouse tower.

"Storm's almost here," Luke said. "We'd better get home."

Jasmin rubbed swollen lips, nodding.

Outside, he helped her into her truck. "Are you ready for the storm?"

"Oh, yes. That's actually why I came by. To thank you. The patch job—patch jobs—you did on the roof are holding. I was in the attic yesterday. No new leaks and the older ones were drying out."

"Good. Now get home and make sure everything's battened down." Luke glanced behind him at the darkness headed their way. "I've got a bad feeling about this one."

Instead of melting into a pile of scared goo, Jasmin nodded and started the truck. "See you later," she said, then headed out.

Luke checked the lighthouse one more time, making sure everything was secured. The rain started just as he got into his truck. By the time he got to the house, it was coming down in buckets.

Oh, yeah, this was going to be a tough one.

Chapter Thirteen

With the storm darkening the skies beyond the normal late afternoon twilight, Jasmin strained to see as she parked the truck under a sturdy lean-to and raced through the pouring rain to the porch, astonished to see her father sitting there. The rain would soon be sideways due to the increasing winds. The weather side of his shirt was already wet.

"Didn't want to be inside," he grumbled.

"Come on. Let's get out of this weather." She helped him up, handed him his cane, and guided him inside. "How come every time I come home, you're on the porch?" she asked as she hung up her own soaked sweatshirt jacket.

He slumped into a chair at the table. "Too lonely in here."

Jasmin's heart broke open. She rounded the table and hugged her father from behind. "You miss Mom, don't you?"

He nodded his head and she felt tears hit her arm.

"She's working hard, so she'll be home sooner than you think."

"Not soon enough."

"Agreed." Jasmin tapped her father's ball cap as she stood and then glanced outside. Rain was coming down in torrents now. "I'd better go check on the horses."

"It's raining too hard. Give it a bit until it eases," he said.

Still cold and soaked, Jasmin gave in and chose to warm up for a while first. Grabbing a dry shirt for her dad, she put leftover casserole in the oven to warm up while he changed. She made a salad and set a plate in front of her father. He eyed it, then looked up at her. "I don't eat salad."

"There's always a first time. Besides, do you want Mom to outdo you in the health department?"

He harrumphed and picked up his fork, continuing to give his salad the stink eye. "First and last," he grumbled, taking a bite.

Jasmin hid her smile as she made her own plate and joined him. She had to give the man credit. He made it halfway through before he said, "Bah!" and abandoned the salad for the sausage casserole she'd pulled from the oven. His demeanor lightened significantly as he bit into the casserole. "Now this is more like it."

Artery-clogging, more like. Jasmin took a bite of the casserole. Her plate was mostly salad because if she ate like her parents did, she'd double in size. Why neither of them did was a mystery to her.

By the time they'd finished dinner, night had fallen and the rain had not let up.

"I'm going to bed," her father said. "Been a long day and I'm tired."

"Okay, Dad." Jasmin kissed his cheek. "If you get up and I'm not here, I went to check on the horses."

"You be careful out there. It's blowing pretty hard."

"Raining buckets, too."

A split-second's light crackled through their windows. Not far behind it, thunder clapped.

"The eye of the storm must be close," Jasmin said. "Good luck with that sleeping."

Her father chuckled and limped out of the kitchen, leaving his cane hooked on the chair he'd been sitting in. Jasmin shook her head and turned to do the dishes. Once finished, she pulled on her rain slicker and went outside. The wind whipped the screen door out of her hands, slamming it against the house. "Oops. Sorry, Dad."

After wrestling the screen closed, Jasmin pulled on her rubber boots and slogged her way across the soggy yard to the barn. Another flash of lightning, followed by a clap of thunder. From outside, she could already hear kicks against stall doors. From more than one horse. Oh, yeah, they were spooked, and Jasmin had a pretty good idea she'd be spending the night in the barn. This storm seemed unprecedented.

She unlatched the barn door, trying to shift it just enough to slip inside. No such luck. It whipped out of her hands and banged against the barn, startling the horses even further. "Damn," Jasmin said, fighting the door, trying to get it to closed. Suddenly, strong hands covered hers. She glanced up.

"Luke."

"Get inside," he said, grunting as he pulled on the door.

Jasmin backstepped into the barn while Luke closed the doors. He threw the bar across its braces as soon as the two sides met. He and Jasmin leaned against the now-closed doors, unmindful of the freaked-out horses for the moment while they caught their breath.

"Thanks. You saved my ass," Jasmin said.

Luke tipped his imaginary hat. "Always up to help a woman in distress, ma'am."

His antics made Jasmin smile. This stuff, the camaraderie between them, she loved. Always had. Until he'd left. Then she'd left and neither of them had come home the same person. Her smile died and she pushed away from the door. "Time to calm the rabid animals."

For the next hour, she and Luke worked as an organically efficient team, calming horses, mucking out stalls, and doling out clean hay and treats. Every time the wind gusted, they had to start down the row all over again, soothing them with voices and pats. When they met at the end of the stalls, Jasmin took a moment to really look at Luke. He was tired, and something more. Edgy, ready to crawl out of his skin. Was the storm affecting him as well? She wanted to ask him. Wanted to find out what had caused his PTSD.

"Luke?"

"Hmmm?" He kept looking around, watching shadows.

"Are you— "

Bam!!!

Whatever hit the barn, it had to be big. The whole front of the building rattled. Before Jasmin could react, Luke grabbed her around the waist and hauled her into an empty stall. His eyes were wild with sharp-edged fear and he searched for danger in every corner, his head on constant rotation.

"Something hit the barn."

He didn't answer her. Hell, it was more like he didn't even hear her. Jasmin tried to maneuver in front of him, but he barked at her.

"Stay back. We don't know what's out there."

Okay, now he was really freaking her out. "Luke, look at me."

Again, she got no answer. Jasmin glared at his back for a long moment, trying to figure out the best thing to do. She decided to wrap her arms around him from behind, hugging him as tight as she could.

Luke went ramrod stiff.

"It's all right, Luke. There's no danger. It's just wind.

I'm here. We're safe. You're safe." She kept talking to him. The words weren't important. Her voice was. She needed to soothe him, help him get out of the war zone and back to reality.

"Look at the horses, Luke." After a long moment, he turned and glanced down the row of stalls.

"See how calm they are? The storm isn't bothering them anymore. In fact, I think it's lessened. You helped me get the door shut and calm the horses down. Now it's my turn to calm you. Let it go. There's no danger."

Jasmin kept a tight hold on him and his hands snaked up to cover hers. Suddenly, so suddenly she didn't have time to react, he slumped against her and they both fell backward onto the soft hay. Somehow, Luke ended up beside her, his arm beneath her neck, the wildness gone from his eyes, though remnants of fear remained. Jasmin raised a hand to cup his cheek.

"I've got you," she whispered.

"Actually," he said, voicing words for the first time since the thunder had clapped over their heads, "I think I've got you."

He lowered his head, stopping a mere breath from her lips. "You are so fucking beautiful." He kissed her with tender reverence, stripping any lingering doubt from Jasmin's mind and laying her soul bare. She wanted him as much as he wanted her. Jasmin kissed him with an abandon she'd never known before. His tongue touched her lips and she opened for him, whimpering with a need she could no longer repress. She wanted this more than anything. Jasmin ran her hands through his hair, pulled him in tighter.

When he broke the kiss, she tried to bring him back to her. "Don't worry," he said. "We're not done." He stared into her eyes, his own a mirror of the emotion and need that coursed through her. Serious. Focused only on her. There was no storm raging except the one inside their bodies. The horses disappeared in that storm, leaving just the two of them.

Luke ran a hand over her hair. "So fucking beautiful." He kissed the corner of her mouth, her cheek, worked his way to her throat. Jasmin sighed, turning her head so he'd continue, causing Luke's need to jerk against her leg. She raked a hand through his hair, throwing her other hand above her head, giving him total access to quench the fire rising inside her.

He took everything she offered him. His hand snuck beneath her t-shirt and up to nipples tight with the craving to be touched. He took his time, damn it, wandering around the edges of her breasts. First one, then the other. Never cupping, never brushing tips that needed his touch. Jasmin arched into him, begging him with her body.

With a chuckle, Luke backed off.

"No," she begged.

"Just long enough to get out of some clothes, darling."

Oh, good idea. She sat up, ready to yank off her t-shirt. Luke stayed her hand. "First things first. Got a blanket?"

Jasmin looked around, not willing to leave him for one moment. "There, on the stall across from us. It's clean. Enough."

Luke went for the blanket. When he turned around, he froze, staring at her.

"What?" She reached to pull straw from her hair.

"Have I mentioned how beautiful you are, Jazz?"

A slow smile spread across her face and she held out her arms. "Come and show me."

When Luke placed the blanket beneath them, Jasmin moved to lay down, but he shook his head. "I've waited so long for this. I want to take my time." He knelt beside her and reached for the edge of her t-shirt, running his hands lightly over her stomach, causing goosebumps to rise. Slowly, way too slowly for Jasmin's peace of mind, he raised the t-shirt up and over her head, branding her everywhere his hands touched.

He lay her back on the blanket, settling beside her, his eyes aglow with admiration as his hands roamed. Finally, his thumb grazed her nipple and she came off the blanket as the sizzle shot straight through her.

"I love how you show me you like it," he murmured, lowering his head to her other breast. He paid excruciating attention to both of them, hand and mouth working in unison to drive her crazy. When Jasmin thought she couldn't take any more, he grazed her with his teeth and she cried out as an orgasm rolled through her.

Luke stopped, only briefly. Long enough to shuck her boots and pants and his clothes. When he lay beside her again, Jasmin cupped him, satisfied when he gasped. He twitched beneath her and she wrapped her hands around him, scooting up on an elbow and forcing him to his back.

"My turn," she said, kissing him. As he'd done, she marked trails with her lips. To his neck, his throat, circling his nipples and sucking them in. Luke squirmed beneath her ministrations, making her feel a heady power.

Her hands moved up and down his shaft as she kissed her way lower, following the line of hair until he thrust his hips up and she took him in her mouth.

"Damn, woman. You're killing me."

"Welcome to my world," she mumbled, then proceeded to send him to the edge. She retreated and advanced, keeping him right there and ready.

Suddenly, Luke grabbed her and flipped her onto her back. "Can't take any more," he said, then froze. Again.

"What?" Jasmin breathed.

"No condom."

"I'm on the pill. And I was tested before I came home. Haven't been with anyone since."

"Mmm, good. I'm clean too."

She wiggled her hips beneath his, inviting him in. That was all Luke needed. He plunged inside her. It was her turn to gasp as he filled her completely.

"You all right?"

"So much more than all right." She pulled him down for a kiss, which he broke off to pay more attention to her breasts.

When he moved inside her, everything in Jasmin's life coalesced into this one perfect moment. It felt so right. He felt so right. She wrapped her legs around him, urging him to go faster, to take them both over the edge. When he reached in to touch her with his hand, she felt the upward spiral burst forth as climax took her. Right there with her, Luke shouted her name as he came.

Jasmin floated on an ethereal cloud as her body relaxed, completely and utterly sated. So much had changed with them over the years. Not this, except maybe that her reaction was stronger than ever. As her body purred, she closed her eyes to revel in the feeling. Luke moved beside her, pulling her into his arms. She drifted off, safe, sated, and more in love with Luke than ever.

~~~

Luke held Jasmin in his arms as she slept, unable to coherently put words to the emotions racing through him. He loved her like sunshine, all his happiness wrapped up in her. He knew that now. He could never leave her, not without destroying his life in the process. She'd rocked his world. No different than that summer after high school. She'd taken him back to a time when he'd been happy. Before life had shown him its seedy, dark side. Before he'd done things...

This amazing woman didn't deserve to be stuck with a wounded soul like him, but he didn't have the strength to leave her. Jasmin was his whole life and always would be. He couldn't fight it any longer. This meant he had to take a good, long look at how to get past his PTSD. No more trying to deal with it himself, alone in the dark of night when the dreams came to remind him of what he'd done.

Tomorrow, he'd call Veterans Affairs and see what help was available. Jasmin deserved a whole man, not some shell who freaked out at every single surprise. The decision added one more layer to his contentedness. They could make this work. He could do this.

He snugged the edges of the blanket over them and pulled Jasmin in tighter to keep her warm. Satisfied like he hadn't been in years, Luke closed his eyes. He'd lay here for a while just enjoying the moment, then wake Jasmin. Maybe make love again.

Rain still pummeled the roof, though he hadn't heard any thunder or seen the flash of lightning since he'd first kissed her. Things had quieted down so maybe the storm had moved inland. Good, he thought as he drifted off to sleep.

Chapter Fourteen

Flailing arms yanked Jasmin out of a sound sleep. Where was she? More importantly, who was hitting her? She raised her arms to shield herself, recognizing Luke's voice in a string of frantic jumbled words. She was in the barn. With Luke. And judging by the way he contorted his body and the anguish in his voice, he was having one hell of a nightmare.

"Luke, wake up."

He thrashed more, then grabbed both her arms, holding tight. "Run!" he screamed. "Get away!"

"Luke, please, wake up. You're having a nightmare." A pretty bad one, too. Unable to wake him up from whatever hell he was mired in, Jasmin pulled free from his grip, got to her knees, and grabbed for both his arms. She pulled them into his body, then she lay on top of him. There was no other way to stop his movement.

Even with her weight on top of him, he flailed and shouted. It took longer than she expected for him to calm down. Tears wet both their cheeks as she held him, his misery soaking into her soul like a poisoned knife.

"It's all right, Luke. I've got you." She talked to him in low, soothing tones until he'd calmed completely. Without ever waking up he wrapped his arms around her, turned on his side, and pulled her tight into his chest. Jasmin listened to his even, quiet breathing for a long time, trying to make sense of what had just happened. This must be related to his time overseas. PTSD was real and if Luke was suffering from it, he needed help. Maybe he was already in therapy but just hadn't told her. Either way, she planned to ask him about it in the morning. What little research she'd done had scared the hell out of her. Too many had succumbed to PTSD. Too many had resorted to suicide.

The idea of losing Luke to his past overwhelmed Jasmin. They'd just found each other again. She couldn't lose him. She lay there, holding him, finding solace in his calm breathing. By the quiet outside and the calm nickers of the horses, the storm must have passed on. She could go to the house now, but no way would she leave Luke after what had just happened. They needed to talk and she planned to do exactly that as soon as he woke up. Not now, though. Morning would come soon enough. She pulled the blanket back over them and lay there for a long time before sleep overtook her.

~~~

Light filtered in through Jasmin's closed eyelids as she came to awareness. She was in the barn. With Luke. A slow smile spread across her face as she remembered the ferocity of the storm and what had happened in this very spot. Stretching her arms high overhead, the rest of the night crashed into her conscious mind. Luke's nightmare. Jasmin sat up. She opened her eyes to find no sign of Luke. She pulled the blanket—still steeped in his scent—around her naked body.

He'd left her.

No small talk, nothing. Why would Luke do that?

Clutching the blanket tight, Jasmin gave into the pain, let it wash over her. Apparently, not much had changed. He hadn't been able to get enough of her after high school, right up until he'd gone into the Marines.

He'd left her, and Jasmin had no idea why. Was PTSD the nightmare or was it her?

Back then, they'd been good together, in bed and out. Had too much time passed for them to recapture that? Things had been so topsy-turvy for both of them since she'd returned home. Happy one minute, frustrated or angry the next. Maybe they were trying to fix something broken beyond repair. Last night shouldn't have happened, because now Jasmin yearned for more. And she'd need to grieve this loss all over again. Hanging her head, she let everything wash over her. Gave into the melancholy. She counted to ten, then got dressed, folded the blanket neatly, and placed it back where it belonged. Knowing she'd never look at it the same way again.

Time to let that all go. After all, Luke had left her. Straightening her shoulders, Jasmin did what she had to do. She got to work. After morning barn chores, she dragged herself to the house and into the path of her father's knowing gaze. Sure enough, he was at the kitchen table waiting for her.

"Spent the night in the barn, eh?"

"Yep. The horses seemed calmer with me there." She poured herself a cup of coffee from the carafe and added a liberal dose of hazelnut creamer, sniffing the strong flavor that usually started her mornings off right. Not today.

"Uh-huh. The horses needed you."

Jasmin grabbed a spoon and a yogurt from the fridge and headed for the doorway that led to the rest of the house. "Going up to my room," she said.

"Uh-huh." Jasmin thought she'd made her escape when her father said, "Hey, Jasmin?"

She froze without turning around.

"Saw Luke was there in the barn until early this morning. Helping with the horses, huh?"

Damn it. Unable to come up with a single response, she muttered an "uh-huh" in his direction and beat feet out of there. In her bedroom, she set everything down and sank onto the bed, certain this must be the ultimate in embarrassment. Luke had left, whether because he didn't feel the way he used to or some PTSD thing, she might never know. And now, her father had witnessed her humiliation. Oh, to have last night back.

Even in her misery, she wondered how he was. Had last night's horrible dream been a one-time thing? Jasmin doubted it. And even with how he'd left her, she wanted to talk to him about counseling. If those nightmares came every night, he couldn't be getting much sleep, which meant he was probably a powder keg waiting to blow.

Not that she'd get the chance to talk to him now. His actions explained perfectly how he felt about her. She had a lot more important things to worry about than Luke Taylor.

Jasmin finished her coffee then headed for the shower to wash last night down the drain.

When she got out, she checked her phone, surprised to see a text from her old boss asking her to call ASAP. She dialed Tom's number.

"Thanks for calling back so quickly, Jasmin."

"What's up?" What could he possibly need from her? She'd been home a couple months now.

"Have you looked at the website lately?"

"Honestly, I've been so busy I haven't had time."

"Oh, I'm sorry. How's your mother doing?"

Finally, she had good news to report. "Getting stronger every day, Tom. She fell and broke her hip, though, so she's back in rehab."

"I'm really sorry to hear about the setback."

"Thanks, it's appreciated."

Jasmin put Tom on speaker and used her phone to punch up the company website, a complicated one she'd designed from the ground up. "What the hell?"

"Ah, so you just saw the site, eh?"

"What happened? It's— It's— "

"I know. There are no words. Rusty said he wanted to fine-tune a few things."

A bare shell of what she'd created remained. And Jasmin would bet her horse Lexie that the shopping links were all screwed up as well.

"It's destroyed."

"It is. Jasmin, I need you. You're the only one who can fix this."

"I can't leave, Tom. My parents are really struggling."

Her mild-mannered boss let out a big sigh on the other end of the phone. She imagined him raking a hand through his graying hair, his only tell when he was frustrated. Then she heard some sort of commotion on the other end.

"Sorry," Tom said. "Leaned back too far and about fell out of my chair."

Jasmin couldn't help chuckling.

"You could do this remotely, couldn't you?" Tom asked. I'll pay whatever you ask, honestly."

Could she? If this worked out, maybe she could pay down the note at the bank. Jasmin tried not to get too excited, but it was a hard feeling to tamp down. *Focus, girl.* She'd have to get high-speed wifi set up. She could use the barn as an office. Jasmin had the necessary programs, but she'd need another monitor.

"I think I can. Give me an hour to verify feasibility, then I'll get back to you with an offer."

"I'll be popping antacids while I wait, so the sooner, the better."

As soon as Jasmin got off the phone, she called to check on how fast she could get satellite wifi hooked up in the barn and what it would cost upfront.

"Jasmin Powter? You're back in town? It's me, Cade Huntington. I was a couple years ahead of you in school."

"Cade, yes, I remember you." Dark hair, quarterback, all the girls drooled over him. "I thought you went to some ivy-league school?"

"Tried to gear up for med school but it wasn't for me. Stuck it out for two years before I decided to stop wasting my parents' money."

"So you're the cable guy?" That was a pretty big stretch from medical school. Both his parents were doctors and owned the only clinic and urgent care in Willow Bay. "Sorry, that was rude of me."

"No worries. I'm only the part-time cable guy because they couldn't find someone local. I get a killer deal on my own wifi costs, which comes in handy because I make most of my money designing video games. I didn't stop school, I just switched gears and went to DigiPen in Seattle."

Digipen had a good reputation in the digital gaming industry. Jasmin had considered going there herself but had opted for New York, a day job, and night school to get her degree in web design.

"Sounds like it's been a good business for you."

He chuckled. "If you only knew. So, you need wifi?"

"Yes, high bandwidth. The highest you've got."

"When?"

"Yesterday."

"How about tomorrow first thing?"

"Perfect."

After they discussed exactly what Jasmin needed and nailed down pricing, she rang off and called her ex-but-soon-to-be-current boss back. Crossing her fingers, she gave him a price that would cover her start-up expenses and the amount she owed the bank to bring the loan current, plus a little extra to catch up on some things around the house.

"Done."

"Done? You're not even going to argue?"

"Nope. I just need the website to run right. What's your timeline?"

"I'll have wifi by tomorrow afternoon and will get right to work. Until I get into things, I can't tell you for certain how long it will take to set things right again, but a few days, I'd imagine." She crossed her fingers again. "If you want me to maintain it after I fix it, you'll have to decide if you want to pay by the fix or keep me on a monthly retainer."

"Monthly retainer. You set the price."

"Okay. We'll work on that pricing after I get you back up and running."

They went over the financial details. Jasmin would have her money by the end of the day.

"You're a lifesaver, Jasmin. Thank you."

Her boss had no idea that, in reality, he was the lifesaver. After she hung up, Jasmin set her phone on the bed beside her and patted it. Had that really happened? Had she just been handed everything she needed to get Powter Place out of its deep hole? Until that money was in her bank account, Jasmin wouldn't let herself believe it. And she didn't plan to tell anyone until it was a done deal.

Oh. My. God. She wanted to shout to the world how happy she was. To tell her father, her mother, Luke. Luke. Her smile faded. She still wondered why he'd disappeared without even telling her goodbye. She'd held him through a nightmare, given her soul to him in their lovemaking, and he'd left without a word. That wasn't the Luke she knew. Was it the PTSD? Or had he left her once again?

Either way, he'd made a decision, so she needed to make

hers. Luke wasn't someone she could confide in. Never again. She'd learned her lesson and knew better than to go there anymore. Still, it stung. Big time. Jasmin rubbed her chest. Tom's call had helped, but the ache from Luke's abandonment lay barely below the surface.

Would she ever get over him?

Not sitting here on her bed, she wouldn't. Until the deal with her boss was for certain, Jasmin needed something to do. She decided to head out to the barn. Time to turn that room into a real office. She raced down the stairs, grabbed her to-do list and a blank pad of paper, and strode outside to start a new list.

Chapter Fifteen

When Cade Huntington stepped out of his truck, Jasmin about picked her jaw up off the ground. How could the high-school heartthrob have gotten more gorgeous in the ten years since he graduated? Wow. His dark hair was long enough now that it had waves and looked unkempt, giving him the sexy air of a man who'd just gotten out of bed.

"Jasmin," he said, offering a wide, white-toothed smile as he hugged her. He held onto her shoulders, backing up as far as his arms would let him to look her up and down. "Wow, I swear you've gotten more beautiful since high school."

Heat flooded Jasmin's cheeks as she let out a disbelieving laugh.

"Seriously. You were hot back then. Now, you're an absolute stunner."

"Oh, come on. You never even noticed me in high school."

"Oh, I noticed. I also saw who you noticed. Figured I didn't have a chance."

Freeing herself from Cade's gentle grasp, Jasmin hugged herself. He'd graduated as she'd finished her sophomore year. She'd mooned over Luke once they'd hit high school, but had worked really hard to hide it. The heat in her cheeks deepened. Did anyone else see the attraction back then?

Cade chuckled. "Don't worry. No one noticed. I'm just unusually observant."

"And I'm apparently as sensitive as ever." Jasmin shook her head, trying not to get mired in high school memories.

"Come on," Cade said, reaching for his tool bag. "Show me what I've got to work with and let's get you hooked back up to the world."

Glad for the reprieve, Jasmin showed him the barn office and explained what she needed.

"Should be pretty straightforward. Though I think, for what you're doing, you'll want the fastest speed you can get."

"I definitely will."

"All right. I've got what I need on the truck. Probably take me about an hour to get you hooked up."

"Okay if I do my horse chores while you're working?"

"What? You don't want to sit and watch me contort my body this way and that, showcasing what is, if I might brag a bit, one of the best asses in town?"

Jasmin laughed. "Oh, now I remember you. Class clown."

"Handsome class clown, thank you very much."

"I really do need to take care of the horses."

"I'm losing out to horses. That's a first."

"Cade— "

"I'm joking with you, Jasmin. Mostly. Still, I would love to see you socially if you're up for it. Maybe we could do dinner some night?"

"Ummm— "

He held up a hand. "Shhh. Don't answer right now. Think about it while I get you wired up. And maybe catch a glimpse or two of how good my ass looks in these tight jeans. Not as good as yours, mind you, but passable. Definitely."

Reeling from the constant barrage of Cade's personality, Jasmin said she'd think about it and fled to the tack room. Cupping her still flaming cheeks, she sank down on her still broken saddle. What a whirlwind of energy and enthusiasm Cade Huntington was. And he thought she was beautiful? Jasmin pulled her beat-up Seahawks hat down further on her brow. She hadn't even bothered with her appearance today.

He'd asked her out. She'd been asked out often when she lived in New York City, but she'd rarely accepted. No one ever measured up to Lucas Taylor. Jasmin hadn't been a saint, but there'd only been a couple guys she'd like well enough to date more than once. And only one of them she'd invited to her bed. Maybe that had been a bad choice. Maybe she needed more experience. Maybe then she'd have some clue about Luke's behavior. He hadn't called or stopped over or anything, and it hurt just as bad as his wordless departure that morning.

Should she accept Cade's offer? Jasmin got up and got to work, wondering how she could answer all the maybes in her life.

~~~

"Maybe we could do dinner some night?"

Luke's gut wrenched itself into a thousand knots as the words filtered through his ears and stabbed daggers at his mind and heart. Standing in the shadows outside the barn, he watched Jasmin walk down the aisle and disappear into the tack room, an energy in her step he hadn't seen before. The cable guy had done that, made her happy enough to damn near skip. Cade Huntington. Luke recognized the voice.

The heartthrob of every girl at Willow Bay High. A 4.0 GPA student and quarterback of the football team. He hadn't been able to compete with that then and he sure couldn't now. Luke was irretrievably broken. Jasmin deserved so much more than he could offer, but damn if he didn't wish they could try.

After his furtive exit from the barn that morning, he'd wanted to call her. To stop by and explain how it devastated him, the way she'd seen him in full post-traumatic-stress mode at the park. And in the night, when the memories were worst. Luke didn't want that for her, to settle for a broken shell of a man. Not when she had options like whole, happy Cade Huntington.

Resigned, Luke headed home with the tattered shreds of his heart, with the memories that wouldn't stop haunting him, with the conviction that he was a hollowed-out version of the man he used to be. He walked back across the property line and closed the gate. Tomorrow, he'd put a padlock on it and throw away the key. With one final glance at the farm he'd come to think of as more of a home than his, Luke turned his back on it all and returned to his lonely house. He'd come over to see if there was anything he could do to help, but Jasmin didn't need his help anymore.

Chapter Sixteen

Three days, he'd stayed away. For three days, he'd tormented himself. Luke scratched his beard. He wasn't used to it, but shaving seemed like too much effort.

He'd attacked Jasmin. It didn't matter that he'd been in the throes of yet another nightmare. He'd tried to hurt the most precious thing to him on this Earth. God, how could he have done that? When he woke up, he'd seen the bruise forming on her arm and realized it had happened again. His dream had made him lash out. How could he ever apologize for that? She'd seen the PTSD animal unchained and he couldn't face her. He'd tried, once, only to see firsthand the opportunities she would have if he was out of the picture.

Luke left the kitchen counter and threw a punch at the wall. And another, and another, pouring all his hate and loathing and fear into a wall he'd just sheet-rocked a week earlier. He turned and sank to the ground, hitting the back of his head on a now-exposed two-by-four. He whacked it again and again. Physical pain was the only way to forget.

Only this time, not even that helped. God, he was the worst kind of human. Luke raked bloody hands through his hair. He had to let Jasmin go. Maybe, if he could get himself under control… No, he hadn't managed so far. Should he fight for her? The idea of never seeing her again sent his heart spinning out of control, made his breathing fast and shallow. A panic attack. He knew it, but was powerless to stop it.

How could he live without her?

"Oh, my God."

Lifting his bleak gaze, Luke watched the mirage that his heart said was Jasmin walk toward him, horror at what he'd become written all over her face. She grabbed his arm and pulled him up and into a chair.

"What have you done to yourself?"

The mirage speaks?

"How drunk are you?"

He shook his head, able only to stare at the vision in front of him. Dark, wavy hair not held back by the usual ponytail. Dark eyes. Lips that beckoned for his. And a body... He reached for her, but she stepped back.

"Luke, you're a mess. What's going on?" She stepped closer and touched his cheek.

"Jazz?"

"Standing right in front of you." She spread her arms out. "The door was unlocked and, um, I wanted to check on you."

She looked frustrated. Mirages didn't ever look that way, did they?

"Are you really here?"

Her face fell in on itself as sadness overrode every other emotion. Sadness and grief. Jasmin knelt in front of him and reached for his hands. "They're all bloody. Where's your first aid kit?"

"Um, uh, in the bathroom."

When she left, Luke almost couldn't stand it. He didn't breathe until she returned. Kneeling in front of him again, she opened the kit and cleaned the blood off his knuckles with such gentle care he almost cried. She wrapped gauze around both hands. When she was done, she looked up at him.

He wanted to kiss her. She was so close, all he had to do was lean in. But it wasn't fair to her. He sat back, feeling an invisible force push against him.

"Yeah, well— " Jasmin closed the kit and stood, placing it on the table. She glanced around. "Place has changed."

"I've been doing a little work."

She took in the hole-riddled wall. "A lot of work, looks like."

Luke shrugged. No sense trying to explain.

Jasmin took a deep breath. "Look, Luke, I get that you don't want me here, but I needed to make sure you're okay."

"I'm okay," he said quietly, trying to believe the words as he said them. No such luck.

"I wanted to let you know you don't have to worry about me and the folks anymore. I got a good-paying job, working from home. We're caught up at the bank and we'll be okay."

A job, a new guy. How could things have changed so much in so short a time? Luke opened his mouth to ask, but Jasmin cut him off.

"And, I wanted to give you these." She pulled some papers from her back pocket and set them on the table. "Maybe something in here will help you. And if you won't contact these places, please, Luke, find someone to talk to. You deserve better than this."

The pain on her face unmanned him. Luke stood and took a step toward her.

"Don't. Please. You've made your feelings toward me perfectly clear. If you take one more step, you'll shred my heart even more." She gulped in air. "Be safe, Luke. If you— If you want to see my folks, shoot me a text and I'll disappear so you can visit. I can't— I can't be around you. Not anymore. It hurts too much. Goodbye."

Her voice caught as she said the last words. Covering her trembling mouth with her hand, she whirled and raced out of the room. Luke ran after her but stopped when the front door slammed closed before he could catch it.

What are you doing? You're no good to her like this.

Luke put a hand on the closed door, knowing he had no right to chase after her. Not until he had his head on straight. Slowly, but with a clearer head thanks to Jasmin's visit, he went back into the kitchen. Wow, he'd really done a number on that wall. Luke raked both hands through his hair and wondered how he was going to get through this. Then he saw the papers Jasmin had left on the table. Resources for vets. Counseling. Ways to get help.

Counselors meant talking about it all. About his time overseas. About the incident. Luke didn't think he'd ever be able to do that. He sank onto a kitchen chair and stared at the wall. If he couldn't get this out of his system, he'd be broken forever. Busting walls, waking up in a frenzy of fear, drenched in sweat. Alone in his misery. Alone.

He loved Jasmin. He'd known that for a long time, certainly since before he'd joined the Marines. Could he watch as she fell in love with someone else, got married and had a family while he lived his sad, solitary life? All because he hadn't told her he loved her and wanted to be that man in her life?

No. He had to fight for her, Cade Huntington be damned. He and Jasmin deserved a chance. And that meant doing what he needed to do to deal with his memories. He picked up the papers, read through them, then reached for his phone.

~~~

After crying the entire run back to her parents' place, Jasmin climbed back over the gate between their properties that had never been locked until now. When had Luke done that? God, did he need this flimsy barrier between them? She slowed to a walk, wiping at the tears on her face. It wouldn't do to have her father see her like this. Maybe she could sneak into the barn before he spotted her.

No such luck. He stood on the edge of the porch waving an arm for her to join him. Great. Well, there was nothing for it but to face his scrutiny, so Jasmin sniffed and, head held high, marched over to her father.

Whatever had put the excitement on his face waned as he looked at her long and hard. He glanced over at Luke's place, then back at Jasmin. She stared him down, silently willing him to let it go. The fact that Luke had left her was not something she planned on ever discussing with her father.

He gnashed his jaw, then apparently made a decision. "Your mother's coming home."

"I don't want to— Wait. What?"

"Your mother's been approved for discharge."

The heaviness on Jasmin's shoulders lifted and she raced up the steps to hug her father. "This is awesome news. When can we bring her home?"

"Tomorrow, it looks like."

"Oh, Dad, this is great. She can see her beautiful new room now. It's a brand new start." Jasmin glanced behind her. "For all of us."

Her father frowned and the jaw movement started again, but he let it go. Still, Jasmin knew she'd hear from him on the subject of Lucas Taylor sooner or later. For now, she'd take the reprieve.

"Come on. We've got some more sprucing up to do," she said, holding the door open. "And a grocery list to write up. I think we should have a celebratory feast tomorrow night."

"That sounds perfect to me," Ned Powter said. "Absolutely perfect."

With her mind whirling from the changes of the day, Jasmin attacked the kitchen, cleaning, washing, making lists. Anything to keep her mind from wandering. She'd started this day with a horrible feeling about Luke and hadn't been able to keep herself from walking over to check on him. And no matter how much pain that had caused her, she was glad she'd gone. He was in bad shape.

Jasmin loved him. Even if he didn't want her, she needed him to be okay. All she could do was hope and pray he got some help. And keep an eye on him from a distance.

Shaking her head to dispel the gloom, she pulled the eyelet curtains down, not surprised when nearly disintegrated in her hand. They were that ancient. The clock said it was only about 1 p.m., so Jasmin grabbed the grocery list and went to find her father.

"Hey, Dad— " She stopped at her mother's bedroom door. He was sitting on the edge of her bed with tears in his eyes.

"You did such a good job fixing this room up. She's going to love coming home to it." His voice broke as he glanced around.

The white walls, washed windows, and her mother's framed photographs brightened the room. If the fact that Luke had helped dimmed Jasmin's elation, well, she would have to deal with that some other time. Jasmin ran her hands over the floral montage she'd stenciled on one wall that made the room even more cheerful. They'd also brought in one of the easy chairs from the living room, so her mother could sit there and watch the activities outside.

"I think she'll like it, too," Jasmin said. "Hey, I'm going to get groceries and a couple other things. Do you need anything?"

"Maybe some flowers to put in that vase she always uses."

Jasmin knew the vase. Cut crystal with a rose-tinted flower etched into it. "Will do. See you in a while." She grabbed the vase, planning to stop by the florist and have them do a bouquet, then ran out to the truck.

Before heading to Sam's Grocery, Jasmin stopped off at the hardware store. It carried at least one of everything and had a gift shop area that made it a must-stop for tourists. The catch-all shop didn't let her down. It had a small selection of curtains. She found a sunny yellow eyelet pattern that would fit the kitchen window.

"Been a while since you've been in, Jasmin." Betty said from behind the counter. She and her husband, Mike, had taken over the hardware store from Mike's parents years ago. Their three-year-old twins sat primly at a table behind Betty, absorbed in their coloring.

"It's been hard to stay away. Our property needs a lot of work." And she'd had no money to do it until now. Jasmin nodded to the boys. "How do you keep them so quiet?"

"Bribery. And I'm not ashamed to admit it." Betty laughed as Jasmin handed her the curtains. "Sprucing up the place?"

"Yes. Mom's coming home."

"Ah, that's great news. She's doing well then?"

"She's been working so hard at the rehab center, she's doing amazing. Walking, as long as she has her brace and her walker. Even using a quad cane sometimes."

"That makes my heart glad," Betty said.

"Mine too."

Betty rang up the purchase. "Want me to add it to your tab?"

"No, I'll pay. And settle our tab." Jasmin offered a grateful smile. "I can't tell you how much it helped that you let us run that, Betty. You and Mike are the best."

"It's never been a problem." Betty reached over and patted Jasmin's hand. "Not for folks like you and your parents."

Tears stung Jasmin's eyes and she sniffed them back. "I've got a good-paying job now. I can work from home and help Mom and Dad out, so I hope I'll never have to run a tab again."

"Well, if you have to, you can." Betty bagged Jasmin's purchase and handed it to her.

Jasmin leaned over the counter and hugged Betty. "Thank you." As she pulled back, a crayon went flying, striking one of the boys.

"Hey!" the boy shouted.

Betty's heavy sigh told Jasmin quiet time was about over. She scooted out of the store, happier than she thought she could get today. The grocery store was her next stop, where she stocked up on everything and bought a turkey with all the fixings for tomorrow's dinner. Thanksgiving wasn't for another month yet, but it had always been her mother's favorite holiday. "Being grateful is what keeps us humble in life, Jasmin," her mother had always said. So they'd give thanks early tomorrow.

As she passed the grocery store's office, Jasmin popped her head in. "Hey, Sam."

He looked up from his deskwork and smiled, getting up to give her a bear of a hug. "Jasmin, it's good to see you. Everything all right?"

"Everything's great. I wanted to let you know I paid up our bill."

"Thanks. I appreciate it, but you weren't anywhere near the point where I'd begun to worry."

"I know, and I appreciate the grace, but I wanted it settled. Also, Mom's coming home from rehab tomorrow."

Sam, a sixty-something confirmed bachelor, had been a regular at Powter Place until her mother's stroke. "We're celebrating with a turkey dinner." Jasmin pointed to the cart full of bagged groceries outside the door. "Want to join us?"

His wide smile was all the answer she needed.

"I would love nothing better. Been too long. Though, I haven't suffered too much." He patted his growing paunch and laughed.

"I'm glad you're coming. Dinner around 5 p.m., if that works for you?"

"I'll be there. Thanks for inviting me, Jasmin."

"You're practically part of the family, so it seems right to include you in the celebration."

Jasmin left with a lightness in her step that eased her heartbreak over Luke, never far from her mind. After a quick stop at the florist's where a woman arranged bright flowers in her mother's vase so much better than she could have, Jasmin headed home full of hope and plans. Two days of long hours had gotten the website back to bare minimums. She had a lot more work to do, but her boss was so happy with her progress, he told her she could take a day or two to focus on her mother. Still, she'd log in tonight to make sure the stats showed things were still working well.

She rushed home to prepare for the best thing that had happened to her in quite a while. Her mother's homecoming was also Jasmin's. She'd committed to Powter Place and the town. She'd found a way to make it work, and had come to understand that this was the only home she'd ever need.

Willow Bay felt right, and she was here to stay.

~~~

Their day of giving thanks turned out to be more joyous than Jasmin expected. Katherine Powter was discharged and home by 10 a.m.

"Oh!" she said when they showed her the newly redone

bedroom. "I love it." With tears in her eyes, she hugged her husband and then Jasmin. Using her cane, she walked over to her framed photos.

"You should enter contests, Mom," Jasmin said.

Her mother shook her head, then shocked Jasmin by adding "not yet." She'd never left that door open before.

"We're having turkey for dinner," Jasmin's father said.

"Yes, but I don't know how to cook it. Can you help me, Mom?"

"Yeshh." Her words, some still slurred, were coming out so much better than before.

"Great."

With her mother ensconced at the table and Ned never far from Katherine's side, Jasmin managed to wash and stuff the turkey. She put it in the oven, then sat at the table to peel potatoes. After that, she got to work on the salad.

"Don't need that," her father said.

"Yeshhh." Katherine playfully slapped his hand. "Shhhalad good."

Jasmin bit her lip to keep from laughing as her father's head swiveled from her to her mother. "Well, shoot, guess I'm getting overruled."

Unable to hold in her amusement a moment longer, Jasmin let out a guffaw. Her mother joined her. Before long, Dad's lips quirked up.

"Was that a chuckle I heard, Dad?"

"Couldn't have been. I don't do salad."

"You do now." Jasmin glanced at her mother, then back at him.

"Pah! I'm overruled, with two women in the house. I'm going outside." Gruff took a back seat as Ned kissed the top of Katherine's head, then grabbed his coat and headed out.

"He's so happy you're home," Jasmin said.

Her mother nodded, clutching Jasmin's hand. "Me.

Happy. Too. Thank. You."

"You did all the hard work." Jasmin swiped at her eyes, then stood. "Okay, now to get the good china out and the table set."

Sam showed up promptly at five, to a house full of turkey and stuffing smells, carrying the biggest bouquet of flowers Jasmin had ever seen. He handed them to Jasmin, then crouched down in front of Katherine and gave her the tenderest hug Jasmin had ever seen from that bear of a man.

That image stuck in her head while she went to the storage shed for a bigger vase. On the way back, she heard laughter wafting through the closed door. Jasmin stopped on the porch, holding the vase to her chest, her heart overflowing with happiness. Her mother was home. Everything had fallen into place.

Almost everything. As Jasmin glanced at the path between their property and Luke's, the ache returned. She shook her head. No. For tonight, this would be enough. With a genuine smile on her face, she walked into her once-again happy home.

Chapter Seventeen

Luke swung his fishing pole behind him, hefted it, and cast it forward, the soft whir of the line almost drowned out by the ocean waves. The line settled in the water and he slowly reeled it in, watching for the telltale dip of the rod. He hadn't caught a single fish today and, in all honesty, he didn't really care if he did. Drawing a deep breath of cleansing sea air, he closed his eyes and relished the peace of the moment. Or tried to. There hadn't been much tranquility in his life the last three weeks. He'd stayed away from Jasmin, though it had just about killed him. And he'd finally gotten some help, not an easy thing to do. He was a long way from the top of the mountain, but at least he'd started climbing the trail.

The only one fishing on this late October day, Luke figured he was crazy to be out here. Distant clouds streaked his way. Rain would arrive soon.

"Only you would be fishing with a rain moving in."

Willow Bay's mayor, Josh Morgan, jogged up.

"Only you would be jogging on the beach with the rain about to fall."

"Point taken." Josh laughed then eyeballed Luke for a moment, probably checking to see if his mood was aggressive. "Haven't seen you around much lately."

"Been trying to deal with some things." Luke reeled in his empty line. "One of which is that I'm more sorry than I can say about that incident at the park."

Josh waved a hand in dismissal. "Long forgotten. How's the PTSD?"

That was Josh. Direct and to the point. Luke considered his answer. He didn't like his personal problems to be public knowledge, but Josh had a right. He'd seen Luke unhinged. "Not great, but I've started some treatment."

"That's the best news I've heard in a while. I'm glad to hear it."

Luke nodded. There wasn't much else to say about that. Three weeks ago, after that low point in his kitchen, he'd made an appointment. After an evaluation more extensive than any he'd undergone before, the VA had started him on medication and he now saw a psychologist a couple times a week. He felt more in control but hadn't tested that feeling yet. And the nightmares were still there. Maybe less frequent and not as debilitating or severe, but still there. He also hadn't had a drink since starting the meds. Another plus.

"It takes time," Josh said. "From what little I know, change doesn't happen overnight."

"No, it doesn't."

"If you ever want to grab a beer, just to chat about life or hang with someone, give me a call."

"I appreciate that." Luke was touched by the offer. "How's Dana doing?"

"Four months pregnant and finally past the worst of the morning sickness."

"I heard she had a rough time."

Josh's nod was bleak. "It got scary there for a while. But thankfully, she's happy, healthy, and not losing everything she tries to eat. And she's going all out on baby preparations. This kid isn't going to want for anything, at least in the first few months of her life." The grin had returned.

"So, it's a girl, huh?"

"Yes, and Bernie is having a boy. Those two are already making plans to marry our kids off to each other."

"Your kids might have a different idea." The stab of pain caught him unawares and Luke rubbed his chest. Fate definitely had its own ideas.

Ever intuitive, Josh asked, "Have you seen Jasmin?"

"Nah. She made it pretty clear how she feels about me and I can't blame her." The bruises on her arm had become part of Luke's recurring nightmares.

"Well, I'm no cupid, but I know from experience that sometimes, clearing the air can be a good thing. Just think about it," Josh said, glancing at the sky. "I'd better get home before the deluge hits."

"Me, too."

"I meant that about the drink. Anytime."

As he watched Josh jog off, Luke felt grateful for the people of Willow Bay. In a way, this town had provided a cocoon after he'd been discharged. A safe place, except from his inner demons. And he was working on that.

His thoughts, as always, turned to Jasmin. What was she doing right now? Her mother had come home, so she was most likely busy taking care of her. Or was she out with Cade? This thought invaded Luke's brain on a regular basis, sending daggers straight to his heart. But how could he begrudge Jasmin some R & R? She worked so hard to keep her parents well and happy. She deserved some contentment herself. He wanted to be the one to make her smile, but he needed more time. He wasn't ready.

A drop of rain splattered on Luke's hand. He realized the clouds had moved in quicker than he'd expected. Either that, or he'd been lost in thought for too long. That kind of fugue had happened to him before.

He grabbed his tackle box and reel and jogged back to his truck, but didn't quite make it. Rain pelted him hard for the last one hundred yards. He drove home soaked, slowing down as he always did when he passed the Powter ranch. He'd like to see Katherine, see how she's doing back at home. The truck wasn't there, so maybe Jasmin was out running errands.

Luke decided he'd go home, change, and walk over to check on the place. To see Katherine. Maybe even reassure himself that Jasmin was doing okay, though that stab to his heart might undo all the hard work he'd done to find level ground.

~~~

An hour later, the rain let up. Luke jumped over the gate, aware that the lock had been more symbolic than an actual attempt to keep him from stepping onto Powter property. It had been more than three weeks since he'd shown his face here. With no little amount of trepidation, he strode through the trees and brush along a path he'd worn himself over the years. The first thing he noticed when he stepped into the yard was that the truck was still gone. Hopefully, that meant Jasmin wouldn't be here. Luke wasn't sure what he'd do if he ran into her. And if she was with Cade. As a high school guy, he'd flirted with Jasmin. Luke's gut churned, just like back then.

Shaking off the thought, he headed for the front porch, aware of some subtle changes to the place. The lean-to where the truck and horse trailer were kept had always been one wind gust from blowing over. Now, a brand new structure stood proud and strong. And the house and barn both had new roofs.

Had Jasmin's new job made all this possible? She'd told him he didn't need to worry about her and her parents anymore, but that wasn't an easy thing to do.

New furniture adorned the porch, too. No more worn couch and rocking chair missing its rockers. Dark brown wicker furniture sat waiting for spring to pull the Powters back outside.

At war with his indecision, Luke knocked on the screen door, finally settling the fight. In a moment, his fate was sealed. Ned Powter opened the door.

"Luke," he said, a big smile on his face. "It's good to see you. Come in, come in."

He opened the door, nostalgically grateful that the kitchen looked the same. Mostly. He knew it was silly but holding on to what he knew helped center him right now. At the same time, he was glad to see improvements here and there.

One of the biggest sat in a chair at the kitchen table, not her wheelchair, stirring something with a spoon in her good hand. Katherine saw Luke and grinned the craziest lopsided grin he'd ever seen. Joy and happiness shone through. His heart lifted to see her.

"You look great," Luke said, hugging her tightly. He found himself matching her wide grin as he squatted next to her chair.

Katherine set the spoon on a plate next to the bowl and patted Luke's cheek. "You too." The side of her face fell—the one unaffected by the stroke—adding a symmetry not often seen on her visage. "Jash not here."

Thank God. "I came to see you. I'm excited you're doing so well." He glanced at Ned, who was grinning from ear to ear. "I think we all are."

"Thank you fur bedrum."

Luke cocked his head, trying to interpret. "Oh, your bedroom. Yes, I helped Jasmin paint it."

"Come. Shee."

As Katherine leaned on the table to stand, Luke's eyes

widened. Once she was upright, Ned tried to hand her a cane but she slapped his hand and reached for it herself. She had improved by leaps and bounds and it lightened Luke's heart quite a bit.

Following Katherine's slow path into her bedroom, Luke looked around in shock. "All I did was paint some white on the walls. The rest of this? This is all your daughter."

"Know." Katherine nodded.

A colorful stencil in a floral design brightened the room and offset the black and white photos that adorned the rest of the walls. Flowers, leaves, park benches. He'd never seen these before. "These are amazing. Haunting, yet hopeful at the same time. It's as if, in each picture, happiness stands just outside the frame." He turned to Katherine. "Yours?"

She nodded, her eyes shining with pride.

"You have an amazing talent, Mama Powter. Wow. I can't even find the words to express how… affected I am by these." He was. Luke walked around the room, past the upright padded chair and table by the window, taking time to closely look at each photograph.

"I like this one the best." He stared at the grayscale ocean, a kid standing there with an older man beside him, his reel in mid-cast as the child watched. Luke leaned in further. "Wait. Is this me?"

"Yesh."

"I've never seen this picture of me and Dad. I remember this day. It was one of the best days of my life, when Dad taught me how to fish. I had no idea anyone else was there." He touched the frame reverently.

Ned took over the story. "You weren't meant to notice us. Katherine and I were walking when she stopped like a birder who'd spied a species never seen before. She brought her ever-present camera up, sighted in, and took the picture, then we headed back to town. All in less than two minutes. Ned put his arm around Katherine's shoulder. "She's that good."

Luke joined them and took Katherine's loosely hanging hand. "You are superb at capturing moments."

When a fleeting sorrow touched her eyes, Luke stepped back. "There's got to be a way to work a camera one-handed."

"We're looking into that," Ned said.

"But. Beach. Never."

"Because you can't walk long distances?"

She nodded.

"Then we'll wheel you. Or, better yet, we'll strap you into one of those four-people bike pedal dune buggies. You can take pictures to your heart's content while we work our asses off pedaling through the sand."

Katherine's laugh was no longer the light tinkle Luke remembered. Now it was more of a harrumph, but with the joy in her eyes, the intent got through.

They moved back to the kitchen and sat at the table like old times. Ned set mugs of coffee in front of each of them. Luke loved seeing Katherine sugar her own coffee.

"I'm seeing some improvements in the place. That roof looks good."

"Sorry to have to rip off all the hard work you did to keep us dry, but we're glad not to worry about it anymore."

"No insult taken. Actually, I'm glad I don't have to climb up there again. At least, not for a few years, I hope."

"Jash," Katherine said, pride filling her voice once again.

"All the improvements are because of her. She got a huge bonus for the job she took, and she can work from here. You might have seen the two satellite dishes on the barn roof?"

"I did. I'm so happy the three of you don't have to worry

so much."

"You helped us out a lot, Luke, during some very lean years. We'll never be able to repay you."

"Not necessary. You're friends. Hell, you're family, especially since my folks died. Anything you need, you call. I'm happy to help." And he was. Most of what Luke did for others, he looked at as paying the world back for what he hadn't been able to stop from happening. But the Powters were family. He'd always felt that way. In fact, at one point he'd hoped to become an official part of the family.

Luke glanced at his watch. If Jasmin was running errands, she'd be home soon. "I'd better get going. Visiting with you two today, seeing how well you're doing, has put me in a great mood, and I can use that. I'm happy for you."

He kissed Katherine on the cheek and she patted his heart. "Find. Help. You."

Not sure what she meant, Luke filed it away to think about later. Ned walked him out onto the porch. "She's a changed woman, Ned."

"That she is." He grinned. "I've got my Kat back." He glanced at the barn. "Looks like Jasmin's home."

What? Luke's head whipped around. Yep, the truck was in its bay. "Then I'd better get going."

Ned stayed him with a hand on his shoulder. "Not sure what happened between you two, but once upon a time, you were good together. I think that's at least worth a conversation."

He didn't make it a question or give Luke an out. He just patted him on the shoulder, turned, and limped back inside, leaving Luke with an IED about to explode in his stomach. He grabbed the wooden post to steady himself. He'd only just had this conversation with his therapist. Could he do it again?

Wasn't Jasmin worth pushing his self-imposed timeline

up? Hell, he'd never feel good telling his story, but she, more than anyone, deserved to hear it.

Feeling sick beyond words, Luke stepped off the porch like a bomb expert moving in on unexploded ordinance. He opened the barn door and slipped inside, walking down the aisle to her office, visions of his guts splayed on the walls hovering in his mind.

In the doorway, he watched her focus on her monitors, so involved with her work she was unaware of his presence. Her hair fell forward, covering her face as she bent her head to jot something on a notepad. Her fingers fairly flew across the keyboard. No matter what Jasmin took on, she did it with every fiber of her being.

God, he loved that about her. He loved her. Luke knew he'd never live a full life if she wasn't in it. Ned was right. It was time for a conversation.

Jasmin took that moment to look up. She froze, her deep, dark eyes not giving anything away. But the stiffness of her back did. She was not happy to see Luke. He didn't blame her one bit.

~~~

Jasmin's heart beat so fast she thought it might jump out of her chest and run for the hills. She stiffened, reminding her errant internal organ that the way-too-handsome man standing in her doorway was not for her. He'd made that abundantly clear.

Except her heart just wouldn't listen. He looked so good. Better than the last time she'd seen him. Calmer, yet she could see the impulse to bolt in his eyes. He didn't want to be here. With a deep breath, Jasmin shored up the wall around her heart and sat back, feigning a casualness she was nowhere near feeling.

"Hey, Luke. What brings you to this side of the property?" She already knew, of course. She'd seen him through the window when she got home and had quickly chosen the chicken's way out, parking and sneaking into the barn. She had a lot of work to do, after all. Except she'd barely gotten any of it done, knowing he was just across the yard. So close, and yet oceans away.

"I came— " He stopped and cleared his throat. "I came to see your mother."

Now that could always bring a smile to her face. Jasmin's lips tipped up at the corners. "She's doing great, isn't she?"

"I was shocked she'd made this much progress. More than the progress, though, she seems happy again." Luke walked into the office and indicated a chair in front of Jasmin's desk, waiting until she nodded to sit down.

"I know," Jasmin said, glad there was a desk between them. If he got any closer, she didn't think she could stand it.

"Her bedroom is so different. The floral wall is beautiful. You did a great job with that."

"Thank you." She'd loved doing that for her mother, though it had taken three days of off-and-on painting to finish it. "Did you see her pictures?"

Luke emphatically waved his hand around. "I' never seen her photographs before. She is amazingly talented. And that one with my dad and me? Wow. I didn't know she'd taken it or that she was even there. He taught me to fish that day. I recognized the brand-new hat he gave me to mark the occasion."

The smile of reminiscence on his face only added to Luke Taylor's handsomeness. Handsome, but untouchable. Jasmin clenched her hands in her lap. This was torture, being so close, yet so far.

"I've always thought that was one of her best."

"I mentioned that we could probably figure a way for

her to use a camera one-handed."

"I've been thinking about the same thing, even doing some research into it. It's totally doable. Look." Jasmin turned to her computer and, with a couple flicks of her fingers, a camera showed up on the screen. "It's really all about the bracing."

After leaning forward and squinting, Luke got up and came around the desk to peer over Jasmin's shoulder. She took in the scent of him. Wood, sea, and sexiness.

"That's a really easy fix. See how it hooks in here and here?" He leaned closer, pointing to the screen. "I bet she already has these eyelets to attach the strap."

He looked at her, his words fading off, his expression softening. They were so close, she could see the faint scar from a childhood fall that his eyebrow almost hid. Her hands came up of their own volition, wanting, needing to touch him, to pull his lips to hers.

Was it her imagination or had he moved closer? A horse neighed and Luke jerked back, leaving Jasmin bereft and wanting him more than ever. To be in his arms again, to feel his heart beating beneath her hand. *Guard your heart, girl.* What she wanted and what she could have were two different beasts and she couldn't live with this pain any longer.

Clearing his throat, Luke straightened and went back to his chair on the safe side of the desk. His face and neck had blushed a deep red. "Anyhow, I think that will work."

"I do too. I've already ordered it." Jasmin couldn't get her heart to slow down. *Damn it.* At least her voice sounded normal.

"Let me, umm, know how I can help," Luke said. "I did joke about taking your mother out on one of those rented pedal jalopies."

Jasmin's mouth quirked up in a quick smile. "I bet she loved that."

Luke shrugged. "She laughed. It's good to hear her laughing again. And the place looks great. The new roofs must have cost a bundle."

"I'll be paying on them for quite some time." Jasmin stared at him for a beat. "Luke, this inane conversation aside, why are you here? I mean, here in the barn." She didn't add *with me*.

She watched his Adam's apple bob as he gulped. He leaned forward, rubbing his hands together. When he met her eyes, the bleakness in his expression yanked one of the slats from her heart-corral. "What's wrong, Luke?"

"I, umm, took your advice."

Sensing he needed to get this out, Jasmin remained quiet and let him talk in his own time.

"I looked through the information you brought over, then called the VA."

"That's great news! You're a special man and you don't deserve the torment you've been living with."

He nodded. "It's not easy, though. I've kept it in for so long." With a deep sigh, he sank back into his chair. "I've started some meds to help with sleep and to keep me from… overreacting."

"Also good."

"And I've been seeing a psychologist for a couple weeks," he said, looking down at his hands. "Boy, that is not an easy thing to do. I sat there the first two sessions and didn't say a word. What could I say? Nothing would make what happened go away."

"I've heard that talking about it can help you deal with the emotions from whatever happened."

"I know. And everything's still really close to the surface so I'm not dealing well. Not yet. But I will be. I know that now." He looked at her. "Thanks to you."

"I want you to be healthy and happy, Luke. You're my

friend." She cringed as she said the word because she wasn't certain she could be friends with the man she irrevocably loved.

Luke closed his eyes for a moment, then opened them, gazing at her with such emotion in his face that another slat fell away from that corral.

"This week, I finally told my story to the psychologist."

Jasmin didn't know much about PTSD but it seemed that this was a huge leap forward. Her smile was genuine when she told him she was glad to hear that.

"I'd like to tell you, if you're up for it."

She couldn't stop her eyes from widening and Luke stiffened in response. He stood. "I'm sorry. I shouldn't be bothering you."

"Please, Luke, sit down." She waited until he did before she continued. "My shock isn't because I don't want to hear your story." Or help. "I honestly didn't think you would ever tell me about your time overseas. You caught me off guard. But I would like to hear it if you're still willing to tell it."

He stood and walked around the desk to stare out the one window in the barn office. He stood there for so long, Jasmin knew he was lost in the memories. Especially when he began clenching and unclenching his fists.

"Luke—"

"You know my parents died while I was in-country, right?"

Jasmin did know that. Her parents had told her. She'd have been on the next plane home if he'd been there. As it was, she'd sent him a long email, the most she could do since she didn't have an address for him or even know if he could get mail.

"Yes. You never responded to my email. Did you get it?"

Still gazing out the window at the far-off trees, he

nodded. "By then, something else had happened that sent me on a bad spiral. I, uh, didn't know what to say, so I never responded." He glanced at her, his lips a grim line. "I'm sorry."

Although Jasmin wanted to dismiss it as nothing to be sorry for, something held her back. He needed to hear her accept his apology, so she nodded. "We're good."

Luke went back to the chair and sat down, elbows on knees, staring at the floor. "Right around that time, I got to know a woman there. We became close."

Despite herself, Jasmin's hackles went up, though she tamped down any physical reaction. Jealousy had no place in this story, at least not until she'd heard it all.

When Luke glanced at her, she was glad she'd fought showing any emotion.

"You met a woman?" she prompted.

"A local. I want you to know, I wasn't with anyone for the first couple years after we went our separate ways. I'd hoped you would rethink things, maybe want to stick around, wait for me. When I didn't hear from you, and I met Aisha, I thought it was time I got on with my life."

Years? He'd waited years for her? She'd cried so hard over letting him go. How had she not known? "I'm so sorry, Luke. If I'd known… "

He waved a hand. "That isn't what this is about. I just needed you to know." He drew a deep breath, in, out, then another. "Aisha and I were together a lot. We'd even started the process for her to come stateside with me after my tour. She died a month after my parents died."

"Oh, no." Jasmin pushed her chair back and stood, intending to enfold Luke in the biggest hug she could. That he'd lost three people that meant so much to him, so close together… "I'm sorry, Luke. No one should have to go through that."

"It was tough. Even tougher… Aisha is dead because of me."

"Luke—"

His hand came up. "Please. I need to finish."

Ratcheting down her need to console him, Jasmin sat back down and clutched the edges of her chair to keep herself there.

"She was a local leader's daughter and the insurgents didn't like her consorting with the enemy. We knew that, so we were careful." Another deep, cleansing breath. "I was distracted, grief-stricken over my folks. Guilt-ridden for not being there. I should have gone stateside. The Marines allow that. Instead, I threw myself into the job and spent every off-duty moment with Aisha. Trying to forget, I guess. If I didn't think about it, it didn't happen."

He nodded, as if to himself. "Except Aisha paid for that inattention with her life. We were in a place we'd found to meet, an abandoned hut just outside the perimeter of the base. When I had to report to my post, I wanted to walk Aisha back to her father's. She said, like always, that it would be too easy to be seen." Luke shook his head. "She planned to leave a few minutes after me." He swiped at his face. "I heard her scream before I got to the gate and I raced back. But it was too late. Someone had stabbed her a dozen times in a matter of seconds, then fled. I never saw the killer. Never knew who did that to her."

After a moment of stunned silence, Jasmin flew around the desk, wrapping her arms around Luke from behind. "I'm so sorry, Luke. So, so sorry."

"Our medical officer said it happened so fast she probably didn't feel much pain. But in my nightmares, she feels every thrust of the blade. And so do I."

Those were the nightmares he was having? "Oh, my God, Luke. How do you stand it?"

"I don't. To think I was responsible for her death. Then, when I realized I left bruises on your arms that night, that was just as bad. I hurt you. I can never forgive myself."

Jasmin kneeled in front of Luke and tipped his chin so he would look at her. There were tears in his eyes, which made her tear up, too. "Is that why you left?"

"I was horrified." He reached to tuck a strand of hair behind her ear, resting his hand on her shoulder. "I never wanted to hurt you."

"They were just light bruises, gone in a couple days. They were nothing."

He gripped her shoulder, not hard, but like a man trying to get an important point across. "They weren't nothing. They were a sign of my turmoil, my lack of control."

With a heavy sigh, Jasmin sat back on her heels. "I thought you left because of me."

"What do you mean?"

"I thought your feelings had changed. That I wasn't what you were looking for anymore."

"Nothing could be further from the truth. You can't imagine how important you are to me. That's why I had to get away. You don't deserve someone broken. You deserve a whole man, like Cade." Luke sank back as far away from her as he could. "You deserve the happiness he can give you."

"Cade?" Jasmin was confused. "Cade, the cable guy?"

"Yes. I saw you two working together that day, setting up your system." Luke waved at the monitors. "You were flirting with each other, and he asked you out."

"You should have stuck around. I didn't take him up on his offer."

"You didn't?" The defeat that had been evident in his voice faded away. He raised his head. "Wait a minute. You didn't go out with Cade? You're not dating him?"

"No and no." Jasmin smiled and moved between his legs, still on her knees, letting fall more chunks of the wall around her heart. "So maybe we can give this, give us, another chance?"

When Luke shook his head, Jasmin froze. "Why not?"

He cupped her cheeks with tender care, his eyes searing the truth into hers. "I love you, Jazz. More than anything. And I can't do that to you. Not yet. I'm not ready. I'm still having nightmares. Not every night now, but more than once or twice a week. I can't put you through that. I can't take the chance that I'd hurt you."

Damn it. Jasmin pushed back and stood, leaning against her desk, gripping the edges tightly. "So that's it? You've just decided we can't be together and that's the end of it? I don't get any say in the matter?"

"I won't subject you to my problems." Luke's face turned to steel. "Besides—and this is going to sound petty but I don't mean it to—you understand when these decisions have to be made. You made yours after high school. You decided to leave."

"I— " Had she? They'd talked so much about how he would be leaving, but had never discussed their relationship until those last couple of days. Then came the Fourth of July. "Stay here. Wait for me," he'd said. And Jasmin had known that waiting for him meant giving up her dreams. So she'd said no.

"You're right. I did. And bringing it up now is not petty. If we are going to have a chance, we have to be able to talk about this stuff. I'll wait for you, Luke. This time, I promise I'll wait."

Luke stood and walked around the chair toward the door. "You should move on, Jasmin. I don't know how long this will take."

"Then why did you tell me your story?"

"Because you deserve to know. I felt helpless when Aisha died. Completely impotent and so filled with rage. I can't saddle you with that."

Jasmin didn't move except to reach out her arms in one final plea. "You aren't impotent, Luke, Look what you've done since you got home. You help everyone! My folks, people around town, so many people. You are a whole person. You just need to realize it. And give us a chance."

The misery in his eyes gave Jasmin her answer. She'd lost.

"Goodbye, Jazz."

He walked out, giving her no chance to argue. No chance to tell him they could work this out, that they were worth the effort. No chance to tell him she loved him, too.

Chapter Eighteen

The convention center had been turned into a kid's version of a ghoulish nightmare for the annual town Halloween party. Jasmin stood with Bernie and Dana, sorting candy into bowls.

"We could have hung those pinatas," Bernie said, as she and Dana watched their husbands.

"I think it's sweet that they worry about you." Jasmin wondered if she would ever have that kind of care in her life.

"I'm pregnant. I'm not fragile," Bernie said.

"Same here," Dana chimed in. "They are treating us like porcelain dolls."

Their grumble had an undertone of happiness that Jasmin envied. Paul glanced over at Bernie and the look that passed between them—even though they were on opposite ends of the room—filled Jasmin with a longing she doubted she would ever satisfy. She hadn't seen Luke since their talk yesterday. And she wouldn't until she could figure out a way past that stubborn, I'm-doing-this-to-keep-you-safe streak of his. They were meant to be together. He loved her and she loved him. Granted she hadn't had a chance to tell him that yet. But he should know it already, damn it.

"Jasmin?"

She looked at Dana, who pointed to the severely maimed candy bar in Jasmin's hand.

"I don't think the kids want crushed Snickers for their treats."

"Gosh, I'm sorry. I guess I got lost in thought," Jasmin said, throwing the bite-sized candy in the garbage.

"And you're ready to take down the world, if the look on your face is any indication," Bernie said. "What's going on?"

"Nothing." She couldn't keep the sigh from belying her statement.

"Oh, boy, sounds like man trouble. You've been seeing Luke, haven't you?" Dana said, taking the bag of candy out of Jasmin's clenched hands.

"What? No. I'm not seeing Luke. Not anymore."

"Okay," Bernie said. "That's it. As soon as this party is over, we're meeting up at Square Peg for a girl's night. Sounds like we could all use a good chat."

"Great idea. I'll call Aimi and tell her to meet us," Dana said.

"Wait. I don't think I can do that," Jasmin said. "Mom's here with me. This is her first outing in a while and she might get tired pretty fast."

"Uh uh. You're not getting out of this," Dana said. "Josh can take your parents home."

"Paul will help him."

"Why do I feel like I'm being railroaded?" Jasmin said, chuckling.

"Because you are. We won't take no for an answer. Though at least two of us won't be drinking." Dana rubbed her growing belly.

The next few hours were full of laughter and screams as town kids and tourists joined the Halloween party. Gladys had wandered in, grocery cart and all, and proclaimed the decorations perfect for the holiday. Not up to dressing in a costume, Jasmin had opted for a wizard hat and a logo shirt from her one and only Comic-Con attendance. She figured Comic-Con's popularity was the reason most kids chose her table to get their bags filled, a great distraction.

She'd kept a close eye on her mother, who sat in her wheelchair taking pictures of the kids in costumes and noting contact information. The brace for the camera had arrived early. It worked well and the five-dollar charge for photographs would be split between the Powters and Willow Bay's charity list. Katherine's face glowed. She was so happy to be functional and contributing to Willow Bay again. Her joy soothed Jasmin's heart.

Once the party had wound down, Jasmin followed Bernie and Dana to Square Peg, Bernie and Paul's pizza parlor. Jasmin had tried again to get out of it, but the women of Willow Bay were forces to be reckoned with. They'd pulled in Connie from the diner, too. She was already standing outside waiting for them, along with Aimi.

Jasmin didn't get out of her car right away. Maybe she could just text that she had to get home to her mother.

Bernie tapped on her window. "Come on."

No getting out of it now, so Jasmin locked her car and followed Bernie inside. Walking into the eclectic restaurant, Jasmin was struck by the feeling she'd walked through a time-warp mirror. Old farm utensils and license plates squared off against modern movie posters and chainsaw-carved animals. This was the local haunt. Tourists liked it too, so Bernie and Paul kept pretty busy. Tonight, the restaurant had closed at six for the party, so they had the place to themselves. Jasmin was surprised to see Gladys had wormed her way into the gathering. She gave her a hug and Gladys tipped her whiskey in Bernie's direction.

"Girl knows how to pour a good drink," Gladys said.

"And I wasn't going to pass up the offer. It warms the bones on a cold night like this."

Once Bernie had poured everyone their preferred drink, they sat around chatting about the success of the evening.

"You know," Bernie said, "Willow Bay had a couple of lean years. Now, with the park, and the Halloween party, and our first annual Beer and Chowder Festival coming in January, I think we're pulling out of our town funk."

"I agree," Connie said. "The diner is finally turning a profit. Good thing, too, because Charlie's out of work again.

"Oh no," Dana said.

"When the weather turns cold, construction dies. It's something we plan for. He worked all summer, thanks to Luke, so we've got some money socked away."

"Luke?" Jasmin asked.

"Yes. He hires Charlie as often as he can and kept him working most of the summer."

Jasmin had always thought Luke worked as a carpenter, not as a general contractor. She rested her elbow on the table and stuck her chin in her hand. She wanted to learn more about the man and his many facets if he'd give her a damn chance.

"So what's up with you and Luke?"

Her head whipped up at Bernie's question. "Nothing."

"Bullshit," Gladys said.

The three other women hooted for some time. Even Jasmin's glare couldn't stop them.

"You're from here, Jasmin," Aimi said, wiping her eyes. "Do you really think these women will accept 'nothing' as an answer?"

"It's the truth." Jasmin jutted out her chin. "We're not seeing each other."

"But you have in the past, both distant and near," Aimi said, reading between the lines.

"And you should be. A lot," Gladys said with a chuckle. "You two are perfect together."

"She should know," Dana said, hugging the elder woman sitting next to her.

Jasmin really didn't want to get into this. "Fine. We dated after high school, then he went in the Marines. Now he's home and we toyed with the idea of picking things up again. But, um, he's being stubborn and I don't have much patience." Her voice fell off at the end. Just saying the words singed her soul.

"What's he being stubborn about?" Dana asked.

"I would be breaking a confidence if I told you, so all I can say is that, in his mind, he's protecting me."

"That sounds about right for the men of Willow Bay. They are all about protecting their women," Aimi said.

"Does that bother you?" Jasmin asked, because right now, it really bothered her.

"It did for a while, but I got used to it. Still, sometimes the town sheriff takes his personal protection duties too far."

"What do you do when that happens?" Maybe this could help her take on Luke and make him see the right side of things—her side.

"We fight. And then we have great makeup sex."

"Shoot," Gladys said. "I can't even remember what that's like, it's been so long."

The entire table erupted. Even Jasmin couldn't stay grumpy after that. Thankfully, the topic of conversation changed to town gossip and never got back around to her.

Dana yawned. "I think I'd better go home before I fall asleep right here."

"Not going to happen," Josh said, walking in the door with Paul behind him. "We hitched a ride over here and thought we'd drive you ladies home. Jackson's right behind us."

The women laughed so hard, there were tears in their eyes. Another bout of laughter greeted the guys' confused expressions.

"See?" Aimi turned to Jasmin, who was using a napkin to dry her face. "Protective."

In no time at all, it was just Bernie, Paul, and Jasmin left in the restaurant. Bernie walked Jasmin to the door. "Look, protective is one thing, but overprotective means missing out. Don't take this from him. If you two are meant to be together—and from what little I've seen, you are—fight for it."

Jasmin nodded, choked up from the love and camaraderie of these women. "Thanks, Bernie. I've—I needed this more than I thought."

"See? We know what we're doing here in Willow Bay."

Driving home, Jasmin thought about what Bernie had said. Fight for what you want. That was so much easier said than done, because she had absolutely no idea how to fight PTSD. And even if she wanted to, Luke wouldn't allow it. He'd taken the decision from her, just like she'd taken the decision from him after high school, apparently. All this time, she'd blamed him for leaving her. Had he left because of her plans? Had he joined the Marines because she'd wanted to move to New York? Oh, God, if he had— Jasmin pulled into the lean-to, threw the truck into park, and shut it down. Hugging herself tight, she rocked back and forth, sorting through her thoughts and emotions, the fear that gurgled up in her throat.

She'd talked about getting out of Willow Bay a lot back in high school. Hell, she'd even tried to get Luke to come with her. Instead of answering her, he'd joined the Marines. Why? Why would he do that? Because he didn't want to be here without her? No. Jasmin ruled that out as the main reason, although to her, Willow Bay seemed like a shell of its former self once he'd left. She stared out at the falling rain as her anxiety grew. Had Luke joined the Marines because of her, to let her go live her dream in New York? He'd never lived in the city. Maybe he didn't want to? Oh, God. That meant everything that had happened to him—that filled him with angst and rage—was her fault. She'd done this to him.

Unchecked tears fell while the misery washed over her. She'd been so full of her own plans and ideas, she'd never considered his. And now she'd lost him.

By the time Jasmin finally stepped out of the truck, she shivered with cold. She hung onto the door, searching for strength. She'd lost everything because of her selfish plans back in high school. Karma was certainly a bitch.

And so far, Jasmin hadn't found a single way to kick karma in the ass.

~~~

From his favorite spot at the top of the lighthouse, Luke watched the ocean. The tide was coming in, which made for more turmoil in the water. Just like his heart. He'd walked away from Jasmin yet again, first by joining the Marines and now because of his own issues. While it had been the right thing to do, a vision of his future, so bleak without Jasmin in it, threatened to overwhelm him. He hadn't slept last night, so he'd come here this morning hoping to find some peace. No such luck.

"Ahoy in the lighthouse!" Luke glanced down to see Jackson Smith, Willow Bay's sheriff, standing at the base of the lighthouse.

"Mind if I come up?" he shouted. Luke waved him up.

"What are you doing here, Sheriff?" Luke asked, once the man had ascended the steep staircase.

Huffing and puffing, Jackson held up a finger, signaling for Luke to give him a minute. Once he'd caught his breath, he laughed. "How often do you do this climb?"

"Once or twice a week."

"I thought I was in shape, but maybe I need to do more stairs, eh? I saw the lighthouse was open and thought I'd check it out."

"You've never been here before?"

"Never been inside, or up here. This is a great view."

"It is. How's Aimi doing?" Aimi had recently moved to town and was their new resident attorney. Jackson, who'd provided her protection detail after a deranged madman took after her, liked to say he'd worn her down until she'd fallen in love with him. Except the way he doted on her, Luke thought it might have been the other way around.

"Heavy into wedding plans. I think it's going to be much larger than either of us want, but her mother is a force to be reckoned with."

Not something I'll ever have to deal with. Luke turned and stared out at the water.

"Everything all right?" Jackson asked.

"Fine."

"You don't sound fine."

This was the downside of living in a small town. Everyone knew everybody's business, or thought they did.

"What're you getting at, sheriff?"

"Hey, we've been friends a couple years now. Why do you still call me sheriff?"

"You've earned the right."

"I have, but you'd better learn to call me by my given name or I'm going to start wondering why you're throwing up a wall between us."

That was the only way Luke could keep the people he liked—or loved—at arm's length.

"Or is that what you want? To live behind walls? You don't trust us very much if that's the case."

Luke started to tell him he should mind his own damn

business, but he paused. He'd built those walls because he didn't trust himself. "Got nothing to do with you or anyone else," he mumbled.

Jackson cocked his head and studied his friend. Luke felt like he was under a microscope.

"Do you have PTSD issues?" Jackson asked.

"Hell, man, that's none of your business."

"It is if you turn dangerous."

"I'm not dangerous."

"That's not what you told Jasmin."

Luke whirled on him. "How the hell do you know what I told Jasmin? What has she told you?"

Jackson held up his hands. "She hasn't said a word. Honest."

"Then what the hell made you say that?"

"Jasmin and my fiancée, among others, worked the Halloween party last night. Afterward, the women got together to chat a while over at Bernie and Paul's. Jasmin very clearly stated she wasn't going to talk about you, but Aimi got the distinct impression that you're trying to save her from yourself." Jackson leaned a little closer. "That the truth?"

Well, shit. It sounded pretty stupid when he put it like that. And Jasmin had kept his secrets. He should have known she would. "Maybe."

Grabbing hold of the railing, Jackson stepped back in a long stretch. "You know, I wasn't looking for love. Turns out, Aimi is the best thing that's ever happened to me. Terrified the hell out of me when that crazy bastard came after her. I couldn't protect her. Turns out, she was pretty good at protecting herself. Yep, pretty darn good." Jackson straightened and reached for the door handle. "Well, I've had my say. Shouldn't be butting in, but it is what it is."

"I appreciate your concern. I've—I've got a lot to think

about."

Jackson chuckled. "Yes, you do."

They walked downstairs together and Luke locked up the lighthouse.

"Uh oh," Jackson said. "You're in trouble now."

Luke turned to see Gladys and her ever-present cart, Mabel, heading straight for them, crunching through the gravel as if on a mission.

"I'm outta here." Jackson clapped Luke on the shoulder. "Good luck." With a quick hello to Gladys, who didn't even slow down, Jackson got in his cruiser and got the hell out of Dodge. The glee on his face was damn near insulting. Didn't guys stick together through thick and thin?

"Lucas Turner, what in hell is going on in that mind of yours?"

Time was up. The piper had come for her payment. Knowing he was a condemned man, Luke helped Gladys move her cart beside a bench and sat down next to her. She immediately swatted him on the arm.

"Ouch."

"That didn't hurt you one bit."

It hadn't, but he'd hoped she'd take it easy on him for sympathy's sake. No such luck.

"What's this I hear you broke up with that sweet girl?" Gladys said, spearing him with her gaze.

"We were never actually together," he tried.

"Pish posh. You two are emotionally bonded to each other. I see it. Anyone can." She patted his arm and, with her next words, softened her voice and her face. "You are the nicest, kindest, gentlest man I've ever met and you two are soul mates. What's got you thinking you're a danger to her?"

"It's hard to explain."

"That just means you don't want to explain it."

"I've got some things I need to figure out."

"Well figure them out fast, because you're going to lose that girl if you don't decide quick. She's home to stay. Anyone can see that. But there are other fish in this town and she's got a lot of love to give someone. You don't want it to not be you."

Gladys was right. The thought of Jasmin with someone else put a sour taste in his mouth. Hell, he'd about come unglued when he thought she was dating Cade. But it wouldn't do to let Gladys run his life, so Luke took the offensive. "Why do you even care? This isn't your problem."

"Huh. That's what you think?" Gladys stood and turned Mabel around. Before she ambled off, she reached over to tap Luke on the forehead. "Get out of your head and rejoin life, young man, or it will pass you by and you'll be an old bachelor with nothing but regrets."

With that, she seemed to have finished what she'd come to say. She headed out, pushing Mabel, muttering things about bull-headed men until Luke couldn't hear her any longer. Gladys had a nerve. It's not like she was an expert at opening up. The woman had more secrets than anyone else in town and he was the only one who knew her biggest one.

Luke sat there for a long while, mulling over the two conversations he'd had this morning. Always one to solve his problems quietly and by himself, Luke had now become the town's project. That galled him, that his business was out there for everyone to gossip about. On the other hand, he'd been an only child and now, with his parents gone, the sense of family that filtered in from these friends held a certain comfort.

They seemed to think he was good enough for Jasmin. Even Jasmin thought that. Luke wasn't so sure. God, those bruises. Yet the meds helped even him out. He hadn't had an outburst in weeks, and his shrink said he was doing really well with everything. Everyone around him believed in him, so why didn't Luke believe in himself?

Aisha had died because of her relationship with him. His parents had died and he hadn't been here to stop it. He could have driven them that day if he'd been home. But would he have? They were as stubborn and independent as he was, so they probably would have refused and gone ahead with their plans to travel in their RV to see the states. They'd only made it about ten miles when the rain came down so hard the RV had hydroplaned and gone down an embankment. The doctor who'd called him overseas said they'd probably died instantly, but that was little consolation to Luke. And Aisha, well, she'd been teaching the girls of the village to read and write, something the insurgents didn't like. Would she have been killed either way?

The chill of the day barely touched Luke as he tried to think. He raked his hands through his hair and stared off into the distance. He felt to blame for all three deaths. He hadn't caused them but he could have prevented them. Or could he have? They were all independent people. As was Jasmin. When she'd moved to New York, he'd respected her right to make that choice, even if it had hurt. He'd wanted her to have that dream.

Now, in trying to put Jasmin first again, to protect her from what he couldn't yet control, he was poised to lose her. At least, if Jackson and Gladys were right, he was. And no one argued with Gladys.

Should he give him and Jasmin a chance? What would happen when the next nightmare hit? And if he got angry? Couples had fights, right? God, he couldn't stand the idea of hurting her.

She'd said they'd get through this together. Luke knew he wasn't being fair, that he was choosing without giving her a hand in the decision. She didn't understand.

Except she'd done the research, brought him

information about local resources. So maybe she did know what she was getting herself into.

The only way to know for sure was to ask.

Luke got into his truck and headed for home, knowing he had a lot to think through.

Chapter Nineteen

After bedding the horses down for the night, Jasmin joined her father on the porch, sinking into one of the comfy new chairs. A very thoughtful gift from Tom once she'd gotten his website running smoothly again. She'd mentioned this was her dad's favorite spot, rain or shine. And these seemed expensive. Like Tom hadn't paid out enough with that advance. A week ago, she'd have considered the gift charity. Now, she knew the chairs were sent out of gratitude. And they were so comfortable. She snuggled in deeper, wishing she could dispel the dark clouds churning through her mind.

"How's Mom?" she asked, trying to stop thinking about Luke and what she'd done to him.

"Great. Still tired after the Halloween party last night, so she went to bed early."

She'd been great at the party. It was like her mother had returned from some depressing trip. Every day now, she kept as active as possible and engaged in conversations, helped with chores, and even laughed easily, music to Jasmin's aching heart.

Jasmin looked at her father's profile as he stared out over the yard.

"How are you feeling, Dad?"

He sighed. "Pain's there a lot. Been thinking. Now that your mother's doing better and things are easier moneywise thanks to you, it might be time for that hip replacement. Maybe after the first of the year."

"I hate that you're in so much pain and I agree. The timing is good and we'll be here to help." Saying the word *we* brought a smile to Jasmin's face. She knew for a fact that her mother would help. She doted on her husband.

"Yep, things are getting settled with your mother and me. Makes me happy."

"Me, too."

"What doesn't make me happy is this rift between you and your man."

The change of topic came out of the blue and Jasmin sat up straight. "Dad— "

"I know it's your life, Jasmin, but you and Luke are good together. I don't understand why you can't work things out."

"It's complicated." Oh, boy, was it. She still hadn't figured out a way to apologize to Luke.

"Try me."

"It's not something I can talk about."

"Got anything to do with that haunted look I see in his eyes sometimes?"

Jasmin had seen that same look. "Probably."

"Some things, a man just has to get through by himself." Her father stood and patted her shoulder. "Give him time. I'm sure he'll come around."

When he leaned over to kiss the top of her head, it filled Jasmin with nostalgia. This was how her father had put her to bed every night when she was little. He'd sneak in after her mother, offer her some sage advice to wind out the day, then kiss her on the head and tiptoe back out.

"Thanks, Dad," she said, her smile genuine. "I love you.

Sleep well."

"Love you more. You sleep well, too. Seems like you're burning the candle at both ends with this place and that work of yours. Life looks better after a solid eight hours of shut-eye."

He went inside and Jasmin gazed at the rain falling steadily beyond the porch. A calmness filled her at what they'd accomplished around here so far. Being able to work again, and at something she loved doing, was a godsend. She knew for certain that she could help her parents weather any storm, and she wanted to do that more than anything. This was home. They were home. And she hoped this tranquility would stick around for a long, long time. She needed only one more thing to make sure of that. Luke.

Give him time, her father had said. Jasmin had sent him away after high school. She hadn't wanted to wait. It wouldn't be easy, but she'd find a way to wait for him now. He deserved that, and patience was the only thing she could give him until he was ready. Patience and an apology.

~~~

Unable to sleep yet again, Jasmin had been in the barn since the early hours. The horses had watched her like she was a crazy person cleaning their stalls at the crack of dawn. Maybe she was. She'd also managed a couple of hours of web-design work. Concentration hadn't been easy, but she'd done it. Her boss had texted her yesterday about a prospective client. The company was bigger than his and she only had a week to turn in a proposal. That wasn't much time to design at least two options and think through the specifics for pricing. Her maintenance charges would remain the same, but design was different with each project and required a microscopic dissection of the client's needs to price it right.

Jasmin stretched when her back and neck complained about being hunched over too long. She got up and looked out the window at the gray fall day. Some would say it was dull and uninviting, but she had always enjoyed the colder months here. Hibernating indoors. During the winter of her junior year in high school, she'd found her passion—designing websites. She was good at it, too. And now, having come home, she could soon be making more money than she had at her job in New York. She'd learned a lot from that place, but it was time to spread her wings to the oceans of possibilities. At least job-wise, she could explore.

Heart-wise, she was still in limbo. Jasmin wandered out of the office. She checked on each of the horses and gave them carrots she kept in the office fridge. She'd fed them earlier than usual so a little treat wouldn't hurt. When she got to the empty stall, she paused. The blanket she and Luke had lain on still hung over the side of the stall. She picked it up and sat down in the hay, hugging it tight. She wanted to go find Luke and apologize, but so far, she'd chickened out. Instead, she tormented herself. How was she going to get through life without Luke? Jasmin didn't think a heart could physically hurt from an emotional blow, but hers ached so bad she kept rubbing her chest. Tears welled in her eyes and she let them fall. She'd apologize, then leave him to heal like he should. She owed him that. You have to grieve losses, right? Well, this one was pretty huge as losses went. She didn't know how she would survive it.

She sat there, hugging the blanket and rocking, thinking about all the times she'd spent with Luke. He'd been so shy in high school he hadn't asked her out until just before graduation. They'd been inseparable right up until he'd left. If she'd told him she'd wait for him, would things be different now? Luke said he'd come home a different man, so maybe, maybe not. But she should have waited for him. Shouldn't have been so stuck on her own plans that she didn't see what was right in front of her. How could she let a man with his heart—his amazing, kind, loving soul—go off to war with that heart broken? That had to taint his perception of her now, didn't it? Tears fell unchecked as she studied their time together. When things were good, they were awesome. Why couldn't Luke enjoy the awesome? Was that part of the PTSD, that he couldn't let himself be happy?

Daisy whinnied and Jasmin looked up to see Luke standing in front of her. She whipped her tear-streaked face away from him and tried to swipe at her cheeks. He didn't give her the chance. He sat beside her, gently pulled the blanket from her, set it aside, then pulled her into his arms. The dam broke and Jasmin cried long and hard, wishing for so much she might never have. Things like this. Luke, consoling her. Helping her through the tough stuff as well as day-to-day life. And her helping him. It ached even more being in his arms, knowing this was probably the last time. She couldn't stop herself. Couldn't stop crying, couldn't stop clinging to Luke like the emotional lifeline he was for her.

Luke had been talking for a while in hushed tones, but Jasmin hadn't comprehended a word. Now, he set her back from him. She tried to hide her face, but he would have none of it. He tipped her chin up so she'd look at him.

Fine. If this was their final goodbye, she'd take it like a Powter. Jasmin straightened and tried to wipe all emotion from her face.

"Don't do that," Luke said, worry in his eyes.

"Don't do what?" She sniffed.

"Don't look like the world is ending when I'm telling you that I love you and I think we need to talk about this, about how stupid I've been."

He loved her. Right. But that wasn't enough, was it? Wait, what had he said?

"What did you just say?"

"Oh, good," Luke said with a timid smile. "You didn't

hear me. I thought maybe I'd waited too long and had ruined things between us."

"Waited too long for what?" Jasmin's ears had to be playing tricks on her. Luke actually sounded happy.

"For us. Jazz, I'm sorry. I've been a world-class heel, thinking of myself instead of you. Or, more accurately, us."

"But you're not the fool. I am. Back after high school, I never should have talked so much about New York and moving away. I pushed you right into the Marines and look what happened because of it." She covered her eyes as fresh tears fell. "It's all my fault. Everything you've gone through."

"Shh, shh, shh." Luke tucked her into his chest again. "It's not your fault. Not at all."

"You joined because of me. So I'd follow my dream."

He hugged her tight, his chin resting on her head. "I did. But I re-upped. Not because of you, but because of what it meant to me. It's not your fault."

"So you're saying I should let go of my guilt?" A glimmer of hope snuck into her soul as she squeezed him.

"Yes. I guess I'm saying I need to let go of mine, too. It won't be easy."

They sat that way for a few long beats. Luke's arms kept Jasmin from falling apart. His touch lessened the ache in her heart.

When she felt calm enough to look him in the eye, she pulled back. "Maybe, instead of staying away from each other for the good of each other, what we need to do is shore each other up," she said. "Work through this together."

She licked her dry lips and waited for fate's—and Luke's—answer.

Luke's eyes dipped for a moment. He reached for both her hands, holding them with tender care. "I couldn't stand it if I hurt you, Jazz. It would be the end of me."

"You must think I'm weak and a coward if you think

PTSD would keep me from wanting to be with you."

"I never gave you enough credit," Luke said, his eyes now locked on hers. "I apologize for that, too. But mostly, I'm sorry I did this to you." He ran a thumb across her drying cheeks. "I never, ever wanted to hurt you. I love you."

Jasmin ran her fingers over the worry lines in his forehead, then down the side of his face and over his lips. He shivered beneath her fingers.

"I love you, too," she said.

"I want to be with you. Now and forever."

Was this really happening? Hope wedged open her soul a little further. "Are you sure? What's changed?"

"More sure than I've ever been about anything. And I've changed. I am changing. I'm better now than I was even two weeks ago. I'll continue to improve. I wanted to protect you but it turns out, you're pretty good at taking care of yourself. I've realized there's no good reason to be alone. I think, on some level, I was punishing myself."

"You weren't responsible for your parents or Aisha."

"And you aren't responsible for my PTSD. It's harder to get the heart to believe that than the mind, but I'm working on it. And I don't want to work on it alone. Jasmin, you captured my heart in high school. That has never changed. Not when I went into the Marines, and not now."

"From here on out, you need to tell me what's going on." Jasmin framed his face with her hands. "I'll be by your side through all of it, Luke. That's all I've ever wanted—to help. We can do this together as long as you never shut me out again."

"I'll try my damndest not to. The same goes for you."

"Of course. And I'll try to be more patient."

"I let some things get in the way of us and I'll spend the rest of my life making up for that," Luke said. "If you'll let me."

Wonder nudged hope out of the way and opened Jasmin's heart wide, setting free the love she had for this man, welcoming the love her had for her. Finally. She put her arms around him. "You don't have to make up for anything, Luke. Except maybe all the love-making we've missed."

Luke grinned before his eyes went all smokey and serious as the love flowed between them. He kissed her, a tender tide in a tumultuous sea. One kiss followed another and Luke began that making-up process right there in the barn where they'd first cemented their love.

Epilogue

Luke parked in front of Pacific Lodge, Willow Bay's only upscale hotel and spa resort.

Jasmin kept staring at the hotel. "I've looked at this place every time I've driven by, but I've never been inside."

"I've done some repairs in here, but I've never been to a party like tonight."

"Jackson and Aimi are pulling out all the stops for this engagement, aren't they?"

"That they are." Luke chuckled then leaned over to nuzzle Jasmin's neck. "I like our quiet thing much better. That way, I've got you all to myself."

With a sigh, Jasmin regretfully backed away from Luke as much as the car would let her. "We have to at least make an appearance."

"Five minutes, then we head back to my place."

A place that was reshaping itself with Jasmin's vision and Luke's finesse, just as their lives had been reshaped by their love. He hadn't had a nightmare in the month they'd been together. Luke had continued with the meds and seeing the VA psychologist. For the first time in years, he felt free of the encumbrances of his past. With this new chapter in his life, he finally felt ready to remodel the home he'd grown up in, even if they only stayed there part-time because Katherine and Ned needed help. At least for the moment. Ned's hip replacement was scheduled for next month, which would help them become more independent.

Luke would always cherish the memories of growing up in his childhood home, but the old wallpaper was no longer needed to remind him of his folks. They were always in his heart. And Jasmin had a real knack for home design, which included some very expensive wall removals. In the end, they'd have the home they both wanted to start their new life in, including the dolphin figurine he'd been holding onto all this time that now adorned the new mantle in their living room.

"We can't just stay five minutes. My folks are parking over there." Jasmin pointed. "We have to help."

"Your mother doesn't need your help so much anymore. You do know they're sleeping in the same bed again, right?"

She bit her lip. Luke could see she was trying not to smile but joy won out. "Not that I want to know that about my parents, but they are kind of acting like honeymooners, aren't they?"

Her eyes sparkled when she was happy, one of the million things Luke loved about her. "Speaking of honeymoons, you haven't given me a date yet," he said.

"This new contract is a bugger. It's going to take me at least another month to get the design right for their website. Then a couple months of keeping an eye on it."

"Are you seriously telling me we have to wait three months to get married?"

Jasmin looked down at the diamond on her finger, Luke's mother's ring. "No," she said, gazing at Luke with eyes filled with love and happiness. "We don't have to wait to get married. We might have to wait for the honeymoon, though."

"All right, then." The hint of an idea began to gel in his mind. "Hey, isn't the judge going to be at this party?"

"Probably." She looked at him warily.

"Then why don't we just get married tonight."

"We can't do that. This is Aimi and Jackson's night, a celebration of their engagement."

"I'm sure they won't mind sharing, and everyone we know will be there, including your parents."

"But, there are things to plan. Flowers, a bridal dress. Things." Jasmin was having trouble wrapping her head around this, he could tell. But it felt right to him.

"I tell you what. Let's go in and check out the party, maybe ask Aimi and Jackson what they think about the idea."

"We don't have a license."

"I'm sure the judge would be happy to issue us one, if not tonight, then Monday morning. We could do the vow thing again then if you're worried, just to make sure. Jasmin Powter, I want to be your husband more than anything in the world. Will you please do me the life-changing honor of becoming my wife? Tonight?"

She studied him as if gauging his sincerity. "You're not joking."

"Not one bit."

"Is this why you didn't argue with me about putting a suit on?"

Luke crossed himself. "Happenstance only. I didn't think of this until just now, but isn't it the perfect idea? We can go on a honeymoon anytime, but how often do things fall into place like this?"

Jasmin looked out at the hotel, then back at Luke, a smile spreading on her face. "I'd love to become your wife. Tonight."

"Woohoo!" Luke hollered and a couple walking by

stopped and stared at them.

"If Aimi and Jackson are all right with it. In fact, I'll ask Aimi to stand up for me."

"And I'll hit up Jackson."

Happier than he'd ever been, Luke leaned across the console to kiss his bride. "I love you, almost-Mrs.-Taylor."

"I love you more, almost-husband."

"I don't think that's possible, but come on. Let's see if we can make this happen."

~~~

An hour later, Jasmin stood in the bathroom amazed at how the night had changed. Aimi and Jackson had been completely on board. The judge's secretary, also attending the party, had volunteered to go get license forms. They'd have to redo their vows with the judge in three days because the licensing required that, but tonight, they'd attest to their love in front of everyone. The partygoers had been advised of the impending nuptials and Jasmin stood in the bathroom impatiently while Dana wove baby's breath into her hair.

"This dress is beautiful," Aimi said, standing by and watching Dana work.

Jasmin had purchased the shimmering, floor-length ivory dress for the party, never once thinking it would become her wedding dress. "I'm glad I didn't go with the little black dress I was looking at."

"In the end, it doesn't matter what you're wearing. It matters who you're meeting at the altar," Dana said, giving Jasmin's hair a final pat before considering her ready.

"I can't believe this is happening." Jasmin cupped her flaming cheeks.

"Well, it better," Gladys said, peeking in through the door before she came inside. "And it's about time."

"I'm so glad you're here," Dana said, kissing the older woman's cheek.

"Wouldn't have missed the sheriff's engagement party for anything. This is icing on a very special cake, though."

Aimi and Jasmin both hugged the woman.

"Thank you, Gladys. I hear you might have had a thing or two to do with Luke and I getting together."

"Well, if you two hadn't been too stubborn for your own good, you wouldn't have needed my help." But the sly smile on Gladys's face told Jasmin she was more than happy to have run interference.

"I wondered if you'd do me the honor of sitting next to my mother and father during the ceremony."

Tears glistened in the elder's eyes. "I'd be honored, my dear. Completely honored."

Everyone but Aimi left the bathroom. Jasmin took a deep breath, letting it out slowly. "Yep. Still can't believe this is happening."

"I can. I'm so happy for you and Luke." Aimi handed Jasmin a Kleenex to blot her lipstick.

"You sure you don't mind our wedding crashing your engagement party?"

"Not one bit. You've made us the talk of the town. And to see all the happiness overflowing, from you two, from us... Well, it's a good omen, don't you think?"

Jasmin hugged her, tears of happiness filling her eyes. "I do."

"Okay. I'll give you a couple minutes to pull yourself together. I'll knock when it's time."

Aimi slipped out, leaving Jasmin alone, staring at herself in the mirror. Somehow, a bit of additional makeup and some baby's breath had transformed her. She looked radiant, though maybe it was the idea of being married to Luke doing that. This was really happening. She glanced down at her empty ring finger, realizing that in a few minutes, she'd be wearing the heirloom again, this time with the band attached.

Or would it be? The band was securely waiting for them in their safe at home. Maybe they'd have to add it later. Either way, they were going through with this. In a few minutes, she'd be Mrs. Luke Taylor. Everything she'd always wanted was coming true. Jasmin's head whirled at how fast this was happening.

Ten minutes later, she stood at the back out of sight as Luke walked Katherine and Gladys to the front row of chairs hastily set up in the ballroom. Katherine, head held high, leaned on Luke and walked proudly to her seat. Bernie and Dana walked down the aisle side-by-side, taking their place opposite Luke, Paul, and Josh. Then Jackson escorted his fiancé down the aisle, leaning in and saying something that made her eyes light up.

Finally, it was Jasmin's turn.

"You ready?" Her father asked, looking resplendent in the dark suit they'd bought for the party.

"So ready," Jasmin answered her father and took his arm, then focused on the man waiting for her at the front of the room. Luke looked wonderful in his suit. His short blond hair had been spiked with mousse into some semblance of order and those deep, deep blue eyes shined. Eyes that only saw her.

With her heart overflowing, she took his hand, and together, they professed their love. Luke put the ring, complete with the wedding band, on her finger. Jasmin's eyes widened.

"You *did* plan this," she whispered.

"Didn't plan this, particularly, but I've been carrying it around waiting for the right moment," he whispered back. His eyes glowed with love and happiness and Jasmin knew hers reflected the same.

When Luke kissed her, the room erupted in cheers.

Jasmin barely heard. Lost in the feel of Luke, his lips on

hers, their future now one, she could stand there forever in Luke's arms. Together. Forever. They had embraced the tender tide that would carry them through the rest of their lives.

~~~

Thank you for reading **Tender Tide**, the fourth story in the *Willow Bay* series. While this series can be read in any order, the next one in the series is **Reluctant Christmas** (Digital game designer and cableman Cade Huntington and Emergency Room doctor Grace Benson, who can hardly wait to get past the holidays. If you enjoyed this book, please consider leaving a review wherever you prefer and know that it would be greatly appreciated.

For new release information and news about Laurie Ryan, please join her newsletter, which can be found at www.laurieryanauthor.com.

Note/Acknowledgements

I love horses and every time I go to the beach (my happy place), I am drawn to the beach rides offered there. Writing this story about the people who offer those rides meant I got to do research, always one of the fun sides of putting horses (or any animals) in stories.

Libby Doyle, you make me shine so bright. Thank you for your superb editing skills. And **Cari Friesen**, your cover for this book rocks! You nailed my hero and heroine and the overall ambiance of Tender Tide.

As always, I couldn't do this without my critique team. **Lavada Dee**, **Faye Avalon**, **Sadira Stone**, **Marie Tuhart**, you always help me see things clearly.

Booklist

Contemporary romance stories by Laurie Ryan

Willow Bay Series
Last Resort
Finding Home
Chances Are
Tender Tide
Reluctant Christmas
Operation Ethan

Tropical Persuasions Series
Stolen Treasures
Pirate's Promise
Dare to Love

Standalone
Rudy's Heart
Lost and Found
Northern Lights
Healing Love
(also part of the Holiday Magic anthology)

Women's Fiction by Laurie Ryan
Show Me

Fantasy by Laurie Ryan
Survival
Enlightenment
Birthright
Awakening
Wolf's Call

Bio

Laurie Ryan writes contemporary romance and fantasy. Growing up a devoted reader, Laurie Ryan immersed herself in the diverse works of authors like Tolkien and Woodiwiss. She is passionate about every aspect of a book: beginning, middle, and end. She can't arrive to a movie five minutes late, has never been able to read the end of a book before the beginning, and is a strong believer in reading the book before seeing the movie.

Laurie lives in the beautiful Pacific Northwest, in the shadow of Mt. Rainier and a short drive to beach-walking next to the Pacific Ocean, with her handsome, he-can-fix-anything husband.

www.laurieryanauthor.com

A Sneak Peek at the Fifth book in the Willow Bay Series

Reluctant Christmas

By Laurie Ryan

Chapter One

Five hours into her twelve-hour night shift in the E.R., Dr. Grace Benson was done with people not listening to her. From the old man with dementia, and no pants, who wandered out before she could treat him for a raging UTI—she'd put the cops onto that search—to the drunk teenager who'd felt her up while she was sticking a gastric tube down his throat to pump his stomach. She couldn't do her job if people didn't do what they were told.

Grace passed a tree in the lobby, emblazoned with lights and holiday decorations. Christmas. One more thing to endure.

The nurse's station was, thankfully, mostly vacant, except for the plethora of garland everywhere. Grace sank into a chair, relieved to be off her feet for a few minutes. She slipped out of her crocs and almost groaned in pleasure, not sure how much more of this she could take. Grace's instincts for diagnosing issues were spot on and almost always validated by tests. One of the reasons she'd gone into emergency medicine. But the shifts, especially night shift, got old. Especially when people didn't do what they were told.

"Got a new one for you, doc," Stan, the charge nurse said, leaning over the counter extending a clipboard. With a glance at her weary feet, Grace slipped her shoes back on, stood, and straightened the white jacket over her blue scrubs. "Emergent?"

"Not so much. Probably a bad ankle sprain but 'Mr. Hottie' thought it might be more so stopped by to have it checked out."

Her eyebrow shot up. "Mr. Hottie?"

"Why do you think it's so quiet here. Everyone's checking out McDreamy-who-isn't-a-doctor, and he's holding court."

Great. Exactly what she needed. Some arrogant jerk who thought he ruled the world. Grace rubbed her forehead with her palm. When she'd accepted the job at this small Aberdeen hospital, she'd figured smaller city, less trouble in the ER. Right? Not so much. She'd traded big city fights and guns and drugs for a smaller community's drama and eccentricities. Now, she was subject to a whole new set of problems and didn't yet have a handle on how to deal with them. Which was why she went home exhausted after every shift. And that had nothing to do with the fact that Christmas was less than a month away.

"Get Xray's, then I'll check on him."

"You know that's not how we work here. Doctor's eyes on the patient, then tests."

Another smaller town idiosyncrasy. In Chicago, there wasn't time for doctors to babysit patients. Triage nurses ordered basic tests, then the physician stepped in.

"Fine," she said, grabbing the clipboard. She strode down the hall to room eight. Even with what Stan had told her, she was surprised to see a group of night-shift people, all women, milling around outside the room. Rolling her eyes, she shooed them all off to go about their business. She knew they called her Dr. Ice. That was fine. She wasn't here to make friends. She had a job to do.

Rounding the corner into the room, two things struck Grace simultaneously. First, that the room was much more crowded than expected for an ankle injury, even if the foot sticking out from beneath the sheet looked rather large and well-groomed. Second, her gaze followed the sheet up to a well-fit, long-sleeved t-shirt that had *Jones Snowboards* emblazoned across the front of an admittedly well-muscled chest.

But the thing that struck her the most was the wide, relaxed grin on the man's face as he chatted with the women around him. He should be in pain. Instead, he acted comfortable and in his element. His dark hair and beard only offset the lighter brown of his eyes and very white teeth. Pulled in by the man's demeanor, a subtle extra thump or two in the vicinity of her heart made her place a hand there for a moment. What had that been? The beginning of another panic attack? She hadn't had one of those since leaving Chicago, so why now? Irritation flooded her as she took deep breaths to stave off the feeling that she'd lost control of a situation before she'd even assessed it.

Why was he so happy? If he wasn't in pain, why had he come to her ER? Control, that's what she needed. Control and organization put everything in perspective and kept her world orderly and neat, exactly how she liked it.

"All right, break time must be over," she said to the bevy of women standing around the patient's bed. "Time to get back to work."

They all filed past her, though some did it quite reluctantly and an occasional sigh or groan was heard.

At that point, she had the patient's full attention and

Grace almost took a step back. The man's gaze held her with a power she'd never known before. It was like she'd become his whole world and nothing else mattered. He angled his head as he looked her over. The grin returned and it was oh, so cocky.

"You must be the doctor," he said in a voice that thrummed through her like the smooth bass of jazz music.

Grace wanted to give him props for not calling her the nurse, but if she gave him anything, he'd take a mile. Something about him resonated deep inside her and set her body to humming. Damn it. She needed to control this situation. Control herself.

He watched her, waiting for her to answer. What had he asked? Oh, yes. Who she was.

"I'm Dr. Benson," she said, flipping a page on the clipboard and reading it. "In accordance with hospital rules, can you give me your name and birthdate?"

"Anytime, doctor. Name's Cade Huntington." He added his birthdate, which Grace barely heard, she got so pulled in by his voice. This would not do at all.

"Ankle injury?"

He nodded, still grinning.

"How did you hurt it?"

"Snowboarding. Took a mogul too fast and had to correct—"

He used his arms to show the movement of his board. Grace followed those long-fingered hands, mesmerized.

"Didn't see the second mogul and it took me down. So, you got a first name, doctor?"

"I do," she answered, grateful her badge was turned around. No way was she giving this man any information. Something about him screamed danger and she sure as hell didn't need that in her life.

She moved closer to look at the red and swollen ankle.

Experience said it was a sprain, but while Grace trusted her instincts, she believed in facts.

"We'll get Xray's and see what's up."

He smiled at her, and once again, she envied the easiness of his interactions with people. For her, chatting with strangers didn't come easy.

"Thank you, Doctor Benson."

With a nod of her head, she left the room, wrote the orders and turned the clipboard over to Stan, then went to the restroom. Inside the stall, she sank down and tried to figure out what had gotten into her. Why would she react so to some guy? An ER patient, nonetheless. This had never happened before. Maybe she was coming down sick. Grace felt her forehead. No fever that she could tell. Still, she was sweaty, her heart was racing, and her brain was all fuzzy. Why?

Could she be attracted to him?

No. Grace tossed the idea aside like the Brussel sprouts she still refused to eat or even try. She didn't do attraction. The one or two times she had, nothing good had come of it. Grace stood and straightened her scrubs. Relationships were not her forte and she recognized that. In doing that, she knew how to run her life, and how not to.

She could deal with Mr. Hottie. He'd be out of her ER in an hour, then she could finish her shift and go home to her orderly house and slip into her bed for some much needed sleep. Outside the stall, she washed her hands and nodded emphatically at herself in the mirror. She had a plan and life was good.

Half an hour later, she stood outside Cade Huntington's room, chewing her lip, struggling to take the steps to get him out of her hospital.

Giving herself a firm talking to, she walked with brisk efficiency into the patient's room where four hospital employees, all women once again had migrated to. Grace stared at them all until they mumbled excuses and, once again, slid past her and back to work.

"Doctor Grace, I've been waiting for you to return." His husky voice almost masked the fact that he knew her first name.

Grace narrowed her eyes, which only made him grin wider. Arrogant and assured of himself. Something she would never be and never wanted to be around.

"Your Xray's show no fracture, so this—" she pointed to his ankle—"is most likely a bad sprain."

"Just as I thought. Will you have dinner with me?"

"What?"

"Dinner. You know. Food? You do eat, don't you, Dr. Grace?"

"I—I—" Grace took a couple deep breaths. Used to patients who liked to flirt, it irritated her that *he* flirted with her. "Mr. Huntington, that is not proper. You will refer to me as Dr. Benson. And no, I will not have dinner with you. I don't date patients."

"Good to know you date. The rest, we'll have to figure out as we go."

She really needed to regain control of this situation. "Mr. Huntington, we're going to put you in a boot and send you home. The sprain is pretty bad, so you'll need to be non-weight bearing for at least a week to give it time to heal. We can issue you crutches here, as well."

"I won't need the crutches," he said, the grin never leaving his face.

"You can't be non-weight bearing without them."

He didn't respond, just held her eyes captive with his own. Grace wanted to fall into them, to smooth the unruly waves in his dark hair, to taste the lips that smiled so readily.

Damn it. No. She was not falling for some snake-whisperer's charms. "I'll get your orders written up and you'll be out of here within the hour. Do you need any pain medication?"

"No. I can take ibuprofen. I prefer not to take anything stronger."

"Good." She turned, intent on getting the hell out of this room.

"Dr. Grace?"

Freezing, she couldn't just ignore him, so she turned back. "Yes?"

"I will convince you to go out with me. Just wanted to make sure you knew that."

Her face flaming, she whirled and fled as quickly as protocols allowed. Shoving the clipboard with her final orders to Stan, she went to the lounge all the ER personnel used, gratefully empty at this time of night. Whatever that had been, whoever Cade Huntington was, she wouldn't have to see him again. Her nice, orderly world would remain as it was.

So why didn't that thought, normally calming, settle her now?

No new patients came in for the next while, so Grace remained in the break room for a solid forty minutes. Figuring the coast had to be clear, she headed back out to the nurse's station, still having a few hours left in her shift and not one to shirk her duties.

As she rounded the corner and glimpsed the waiting room, Cade Huntington limped in his boot to the exit, carrying crutches his insurance would pay for. Damn it. He should listen to her. She knew what she was talking about, and if he didn't stay off that ankle, he'd have worse problems to come.

As the door swooshed open automatically, he stopped and turned, his gaze finding her unerringly. With a smile, he waved his crutches at her and limped out the door. And out of her life.

Thank God.

~~~

Never in his life had Cade reacted to a woman so strongly. This time of night, the clinic his parents ran in Willow Bay was closed. Plus, he wouldn't have gone there anyhow to listen to their rants about his life. Cade shook his head. He did not need that kind of grief. So he'd diverted to the closest hospital, Grays Harbor General. Meeting Dr. Grace, though, had thrown him for a loop. What was it about the winsome physician that strummed the right chord in him? She was beautiful. No arguing that with her blonde hair and those intelligent blue eyes. She was also very uptight, something he didn't generally go for in a woman. He'd accepted an unasked for challenge, telling her he would convince her to go out with him.

What the hell had gotten into him? Especially with that parting shot, walking out without using his crutches. Now his ankle hurt like a son of a bitch. He climbed into his SUV and gulped down four ibuprofen without water, then laid his head back against the headrest and breathed in and out, wishing the pain away.

Not that it worked. The ankle throbbed like crazy and he had a forty minute drive to get home. As it turned out, an agonizing forty-five minute drive. When Cade hit the button to open his garage door, then pulled in, it was after two am and all he wanted to do was sink into bed. And get his damn ankle above his heart. He remembered that much from the doctor's mantra.

Actually, he remembered everything. Every nuance of her silky voice, the wariness in her eyes, the desire in him to pull the pins out of her bun and see how long and luxurious those blonde tresses really were. He hadn't been that into a woman since... Well, it had been a long time.

Using the damn crutches, Cade walked through his house without turning on lights. He didn't need to thanks to the Christmas lights he'd put up everywhere on timers. He grabbed an ice pack and a bottle of water from the fridge, then climbed the stairs to his bedroom, tripping on the fourth stair and going down.

"Damn crutches." Cade did the rest of the stairs on his butt, cussing the whole way. At the top, he threw the crutches down and hopped into his room. He wasn't unfamiliar with crutches, but it had been a while and he hated them now as much as he did then.

The ibuprofen had finally taken the edge off. Shedding his clothes, he sank into his mattress, wrapped an ice pack around the ankle and put it up on a pillow. Drinking water could wait. Right now, he needed sleep and healing.

Except neither came easy as he kept thinking about threading his fingers through long, blonde locks of hair, staring into the deep blue sea of eyes that he knew would haunt him while he made plans to coax a smile from lips that were born to be kissed.

~~~

More information about **Reluctant Christmas** and Laurie Ryan can be found on her website.
www.laurieryanauthor.com

www.ingramcontent.com/pod-product-compliance
Lightning Source LLC
LaVergne TN
LVHW021237080526
838199LV00088B/4557